CIRCLE OF THREE

OTHER YEARLING BOOKS YOU WILL ENJOY:

YEARLING BOOKS are designed especially to entertain and enlighten young people. Patricia Reilly Giff, consultant to this series, received her bachelor's degree from Marymount College and a master's degree in history from St. John's University. She holds a Professional Diploma in Reading and a Doctorate of Humane Letters from Hofstra University. She was a teacher and reading consultant for many years, and is the author of numerous books for young readers.

CIRCLE of THREE

TALES OF THE NINE CHARMS

ERICA FARBER
AND
J. R. SANSEVERE

A YEARLING BOOK

35 Years of Exceptional Reading

Yearling Books
Established 1966

Published by
Dell Yearling
an imprint of
Random House Children's Books
a division of Random House, Inc.
1540 Broadway
New York, New York 10036

Visit us on the Web! www.randomhouse.com/kids

Educators and librarians, for a variety of teaching tools, visit us at www.randomhouse.com/teachers

---

ISBN 0-440-41513-6

Printed in the United States of America

July 2001

10 9 8 7 6 5 4 3 2 1

OPM

For my mother

—E.F.

For Shaw and Des

—J.R.S. and E.F.

Special thanks to our editor,
Diana Capriotti, who always
believed in the magic of the charms

THE NINE CHARMS

Nine were the charms,
golden-silver, made of light,
forged by the Lords of Time
to help take back the night.
Each of these nine lords
one color charm did hold,
to fight the darkness rising,
or so the story's told.

PROLOGUE

"She's so fat, when she steps on the scale, it says 'To be continued,' " whispered Walker Crane.

He and his best friend, Henry, laughed so hard they tripped up the last few steps into the museum. Luckily they were at the end of the line, so Miss Hamilton, their teacher, didn't see them.

"Hey, I've got another one," said Walker.

Before Walker could share, Miss "Hoot Owl" Hamilton cleared her throat and the class jumped to attention. Everyone but Walker, actually. Miss Hamilton had gotten her nickname because of her beaklike nose and her beady eyes, which blinked incessantly behind round glasses. And she could sniff out trouble before it even happened, like an owl catching a mouse in the dark of night.

"We are about to enter the Gallery of European Painting and Decorative Arts," she announced. "And how will we behave?"

"With decorum," said Prissy Chrissy, who got straight A's. She smiled at Miss Hamilton.

"And what does *decorum* mean?"

Walker turned to the boys around him.

"She's so fat, when she steps on the scale, it says 'One person at a time.' "

Walker and Henry both burst out laughing again.

Prissy Chrissy raised her hand once more, but Miss Hamilton's eyes passed over her and over Terence and Larry, whose projects won the science fair every year, whose hands were also raised. Walker ducked, the laughter dying in his throat, as he noticed those beady eyes roaming the group, like a vulture looking for roadkill, but it was too late. He had been spotted.

"Mr. Crane, can you tell us the meaning of the word *decorum*?"

Walker frowned, pretending to be deep in thought.

"Uh . . . decorum . . . that is, Deck Orum

. . . is . . . the name of the man who founded this museum." His eyes twinkled as he warmed to his story. "See, he was this great boxer, who loved art, of course. He always decked his opponents and that's why they called him Deck. Get it, Deck Orum?"

The class tittered.

Miss Hamilton raised one dark eyebrow and frowned. *"Decorum,"* she intoned, "is not the name of a person. It is propriety and good taste in conduct and appearance, something which, Mr. Crane, you seem to be greatly lacking. And which we can discuss at greater length when you join me for detention tomorrow after school. It comes from the Latin *decorus,* which means?"

"Honorable," answered Prissy Chrissy.

Miss Hamilton mooed with satisfaction.

Walker and Henry shuffled along behind the rest of the class. Miss Hamilton sure had no sense of humor, Walker thought, as they stopped in front of a wall of paintings.

"And now let's examine some of the most revolutionary paintings of the nineteenth century."

Walker's ears perked up at the word *revolutionary.* He liked history, especially wars and guns and soldiers and stuff. It was his best subject. But when he took a look at the paintings, his mouth dropped open. "What's a bunch of hay got to do with the Revolutionary War?"

Miss Hamilton turned her beady eyes on him once more. "Pay attention, Mr. Crane. I'm watching you."

Then she turned to the class. "As I was saying, Claude Monet revolutionized painting. These are not simply haystacks you see before you. In these paintings Monet celebrated the haystack as a mirror for the unfolding works of light in time."

Her voice droned on about the power of light illuminating darkness, and Walker, bored, let his glance fall away from the painting and down at the floor—and noticed a small but interesting detail that had unbelievably escaped his attention earlier. There in plain sight, stuck to one of Miss Hamilton's lace-up, rubber-soled, sensible black shoes, was a long piece of white toilet paper.

Walker tapped Henry on the shoulder and raised his eyebrows in the direction of the toilet paper. The two boys looked at each other and laughed.

Miss Hamilton turned her beady eyes on Walker. "Just what is so amusing, Mr. Crane?"

Walker shrugged. It wasn't his fault she had toilet paper stuck on her shoe.

"Nothing," he said.

"Then why were you laughing?"

"I'm supposed to tell the truth, Miss Hamilton, right? Aren't you always supposed to tell the truth, like George Washington and the cherry tree?"

"Of course, Mr. Crane. Don't be snide with me. *What* is so funny?"

"You have toilet paper stuck to your shoe," Walker finally said. Everyone burst out laughing at that, even Prissy Chrissy, who clapped her hand over her mouth in an effort to stop herself.

Miss Hamilton proceeded to blush, turning a shade of red that reflected light in ways that would have made Monet most proud.

"Mr. Crane, since you seem to have such a sharp eye for detail, you can write a two-page essay to-night on the significance of light in this series of paintings."

Great, thought Walker. He hated writing, espe-cially since he was such a bad speller. Anyway, light was just light. The opposite of dark. Nothing more or less and certainly nothing to write two pages about.

"All right, class. Time for lunch."

The group followed their teacher to a sunlit court-yard with a bubbling fountain and arranged them-selves around metal tables, where they began pulling out their lunches. Walker, eager to put some distance between himself and Miss Hamilton, led Henry to the fountain and sat on the edge.

"What you got?" asked Henry as he pulled out his lunch.

"The usual. Cheese, lettuce, and pickles with mustard and mayo on white."

"Where's the meat? Why don't you try some salami or ham or turkey or something once in a while?" Henry asked through a huge mouthful of his bologna and cheese sandwich.

"You know what bologna's made of?" Walker said before Henry could swallow and reply. "Let me tell you. It's made of the waste products of other meat. Like the intestines and the liver and the heart and the guts. They grind it all up in these big machines and then—"

"Cut it out, Walker. Don't tell me that stuff when I'm eating."

"And then it comes squishing out onto these big sheets—" Walker continued.

"Walker, quit it!"

"And then it hardens and they cut it into slices and there's your lunch. You know, if you leave one of those slices out in the sun for long enough, white worms come crawling out of it."

“Shut up!” yelled Henry, elbowing Walker hard in the ribs.

Walker lurched to the side and dropped his sandwich into the fountain, where it landed between two lily pads.

“Now look what you made me do,” said Walker. “That’s all I brought to eat.”

He was staring forlornly down at his sandwich when he spotted something shiny. It stood out clearly, a metallic gleam against the black stone of the fountain. Find a penny, pick it up, Walker thought.

As he touched the glowing metal, the wind suddenly began to blow. Clouds skidded through the sky, covering the sun, and the courtyard was plunged into a deep, murky gloom. Thunder rumbled overhead, though no storm had been predicted.

Walker didn’t notice the weather. He pulled the penny out of the water. It wasn’t a coin as he’d thought at first, but a small piece of metal, a shining combination of both gold and silver, encircling a fiery red stone. Walker held it in his palm and flipped it over, watching the stone catch the little light that shone through the clouds. The metal felt smooth and cold to the touch. And old somehow. Very old.

"Class!" called Miss Hamilton. "Let's go inside! Now."

Lightning suddenly streaked the sky. At the same time, the wind began to gust with such force that it knocked over one of the metal tables. Chairs blew over, crashing into the windows of the museum. Prissy Chrissy was screaming as everyone made a run for the door.

"C'mon, Walker, let's go," said Henry uneasily, his eyes wide.

"Look at this," said Walker in a hushed voice, holding out his hand.

"What?" said Henry. "I don't see anything. We better go."

Just then a flash of lightning hit the water in the fountain, so close to Walker he could practically feel the electricity coursing through his body. He tried to stand and move away, but he slipped somehow and fell backward into the fountain.

"Walker!" Henry yelled, stretching out his hand.

Walker tried to grab his friend's hand, but he couldn't reach it. Though the water in the fountain was no more than a foot deep, somehow Walker kept falling. He could see Henry's arm reaching out for him, shimmering through the water. And he could see his friend's face distorted by the waves, but he kept falling farther away through the bottomless fountain as the water roared around his ears.

Walker fell until the water disappeared and blackness surrounded him. The only sound he could hear was the beating of his own heart.

CHAPTER I

The hallway was empty. Shadows danced on the gray flagstones as the afternoon sun slanted through the small slit windows of the castle. Niko slipped around the corner, followed by his falcon, her yellow eyes glowing in the gloomy hall.

"One . . . two . . . three . . . ," his voice echoed as he threw a small brightly colored ball.

With a screech, Topaz flew off and caught the ball in her powerful talons before it reached the ground. She returned to her master and dropped the ball into his outstretched hand.

"Good girl," he said, stroking her crest feathers.

Niko turned into another long hallway. This time when he threw the ball, he slipped behind one of the straight-back wooden chairs that lined the walls. Find me now, girl, he thought. This variation of hide-and-seek was a game he had played with Topaz since he was small. He held his breath, trying to remain as still as possible.

But instead of the gentle swish of feathers, he heard footsteps and the lilting north-country accent of Ruah, the head housekeeper at the Castle of the Seven Towers.

"I'm tellin' you, the Emperor isn't long for this world, and when he dies, the dark one will come again. I feel the shadows slippin' closer and closer."

The dark one, Niko thought. He'd heard that name before, once, when he was small. He'd gone to the master's study late one night and peeked through the door. The master sat at his desk, listening to someone who stood where Niko couldn't see. A glow of green light illuminated the room, and Niko thought how strange that was. The visitor had said something about the dark one. But the master hadn't said a word. He'd just sat there, looking troubled and sad. It had scared Niko to see his master so shaken, scared him so much that he never asked what the dark one was all about.

"Come now, Ruah," said a warm male voice, which Niko knew belonged to Mal, the castle steward. "The dark one ain't around no more—if he ever existed at all. And even if he was here and the Emperor was dead, then there'd be the regent ruling the kingdom, till the Emperor's son comes of age. And you know the master will be the regent and he'll be able to stop the dark one."

"What happens if Lord Amber ain't the regent?" said Ruah.

"What are you talking about?"

"What if Lord Amber's name ain't in the box?"

Niko peered around the side of the chair. Ruah had stopped walking and stood in the center of the hall in her red apron and cap, a small, stout figure with a pale, wrinkled face framed by wispy gray hair. The box? Niko wondered. What box? Lord Amber had never told him anything about a box or the fact that he might be the regent of the kingdom one day.

"Course Lord Amber's name is in the box. He was the Emperor's right hand all through the War of the Flowers, just about the most important man in the entire kingdom of Sunnebēam besides the Emperor himself. And only the greatest military strategist of all time. Only stands to reason the Emperor would choose him to be regent."

Ruah clucked her tongue. "Lord Amber's name should be in the box, of course. But the ways of the dark is very tricky. And just because something should be so, don't mean the dark one can't change what will come to pass. That's what I heard down the Gypsy camp on t'other side of the harbor. The card reader drew the Hanged Man. And you know what the Hanged Man means?"

Mal shrugged his shoulders as if to dismiss the entire business and stared at Ruah with a tolerant smile.

"The dark is rising and soon the light 'twill be gone—for good."

"Now, Ruah, you know them Gypsies likes to tell a tall story now and then, especially for some silver."

"Ain't no story, Mal. 'Tis the truth. I have a bad feeling of late, comes over me sometimes when I wake up in the wee hours. Somethin' is goin' to happen."

Mal patted Ruah gently on the shoulder. "Come, come. We're all a bit jumpy since the kingdom of Kasmania violated our treaty and sent soldiers across our border. Sure they say it's friendly, but with that smooth-talkin' Ambassador Le Croix movin' into the palace, even though he is the Empress's cousin, I don't like it any more than you do. But none of that got anything to do with the dark one."

"It does, I tell you. And them Dragons, too."

"That's all just superstitious mumbo jumbo. Anyway, the Dragons is been disbanded for a long time—ever since Janus died."

At the mention of the name Janus, Niko watched Ruah ball her right hand into a fist and make the sign of the Dragon's Eye, in an ancient gesture of protection—fist to her forehead, then left shoulder, then right.

Topaz chose that moment to swoop back into the hall. She dropped the ball on the back of Niko's chair and cawed. Ruah and Mal looked over in surprise as Niko rose from his hiding place, a sheepish expression in his pale gray eyes.

"Don't little pitchers have big ears?" said Ruah. She walked over to the boy and pulled him gently but firmly by said ears. "Now, off with you and that bird. Back to your studies. The master will be in to see you shortly." Although she spoke gruffly, Niko saw the smile on her round face and felt her slip something into the pocket of his tunic before she hurried him off down the hall. A sweet cake, he was sure.

He heard her voice floating toward him as he walked away. "With just that bird for company since he was a tot, it's a lonely life for a boy, but the master insists."

The rest of her words were lost as Niko walked toward the library. If only Topaz hadn't come back, he might have heard more about the legendary warrior Janus and the Dragons. And maybe an answer to some of the questions spinning in his head. What did the dark one have to do with Janus? If Lord Amber was named regent, would he have to move to the palace? Would he take Niko with him and allow him to start training to be a warrior? It would be different to live in a busy place like the palace after the isolation of the Castle of the Seven Towers, where Lord Amber had lived ever since the War of the Flowers.

Niko wished with all his heart that he could be a warrior like Janus, but Lord Amber forbade him to handle real weapons. "A warrior of the sword must first learn the strength of the pen," his master liked to say. But a warrior of the pen was not a warrior at all as far as Niko was concerned. Surely he'd have to learn to fight if he was going to live in the palace.

Niko didn't see Topaz anywhere, so he turned one corner and then another, whistling for her. Halfway down a hall, he spotted her in a stone alcove.

"One more time, girl," he said as he threw the ball around the corner. He had so many questions and no one to ask. Lord Amber did not like to speak of the past. He wouldn't even talk about his role in the War of the Flowers during history lessons. He said it was only the present that mattered, for the past and the future were elusive, shimmering things that fell apart when you reached for them, like rainbows on a clear day. Niko disagreed. He thought the past mattered a great deal—especially when you knew nothing about your own.

Topaz *cak-cak*ed and Niko, jolted out of his thoughts, looked up in surprise to see that he had wandered into the entrance of the seventh tower, the one place in the castle he was forbidden to go.

There was Topaz, perched on the jamb of the arched mahogany door. Though usually closed, the door was slightly ajar, not enough for the bird to fly through but enough for the ball to have rolled inside the forbidden tower.

Niko knew he should just stretch his arm through the door, pick up the ball, and leave, but his curiosity flared. What could be up there that the master didn't want him to see? Perhaps he kept relics of his days as second-in-command of the kingdom, or perhaps he kept the secrets about the past. Maybe he kept information about Niko himself that he didn't want the boy to know.

His heart beating hard, Niko pushed the door farther open. There before him was a dusty flight of stone steps. Leave now, he told himself, but curiosity held him there, frozen in place. He had never willfully disobeyed the master, but something about those steps urged him upward into the dusty darkness.

A quick glance over his shoulder revealed nothing but a silent hall. Topaz fastened her golden eyes on him, watching, waiting. Before he could lose his nerve, Niko stepped into the murky gloom.

No one would ever have to know.

Niko's eyes widened as he flipped the door latch and stepped into the chamber at the top of the forbidden stairs. Weapons covered the room, stacked on the floor, ranged along the walls, and perched in wooden racks. Long swords, short swords, spears, shields, maces, bows, arrows, daggers, lances, rapiers—more weapons than Niko had ever dreamed of in his wildest fantasy.

Slowly he walked to the swords hanging in long, neat rows. He ran his fingers over the smooth metal of the blades, the heavy detailed craftsmanship of the jewel-encrusted hilts, the gold filigree and engravings. The sun slipped westward and slanted in through the opposite window, striking one of the swords. It was simple in design, silver with a silver hilt, enriched by only one detail—an engraving of what looked like a gate. Slowly Niko reached for it.

At that moment, the door behind him banged open. Niko whirled around and found himself staring into the dark, flashing eyes of his master.

"You know you are forbidden to enter here," rasped Lord Amber angrily. Niko nodded, staring at the wrinkled old face, the long white hair, the blue robe with the hawk crest emblazoned over the right breast.

Lord Amber said nothing for a long moment, and Niko shifted uncomfortably, afraid to speak and anger his master further. The silence grew louder.

"If you wish so badly to handle weapons, then we shall fight," Lord Amber said. "Choose."

Niko blinked, too astonished to move. Lord Amber spun toward him, his right hand gripping a golden sword Niko had never seen before. He pointed the sword at Niko's chest, holding the gleaming blade just inches from the boy's heart.

"You have already forgotten the principle of spark and stone? If the mind rests on the sword and not on the eyes of the one who is about to strike, there will be an interval and your own action will be lost."

Niko gulped. The action of spark and stone was one of the first principles Lord Amber had taught him about writing: Just as there is no interval between the moment you strike the stone and the moment the spark appears, you must never allow an interval between the thought and the movement of the pen to express it on paper. It was the only way to capture the purity of thought before you second-guessed yourself and forgot it. Niko had never realized before that the same principle applied to dueling.

Lord Amber withdrew his sword. "Now choose your weapon."

Niko turned back to the wall of swords, his eye once more drawn to the simple silver one. He pulled it down. The well-worn hilt felt cool to his touch as he held the sword awkwardly.

"Are you certain that is the one?" rasped Lord Amber, his dark eyes boring into Niko's with a look of such fierceness, Niko almost said it wasn't. But after another glance at the sword, he nodded.

He stood with his head high and his legs firm and strong. He imagined strength flowing from the top of his head all the way down to his toes, concentrating on the energy coursing through his body. He would show Lord Amber just how good a fighter he could be. He would prove that he was ready for a sword of his own.

Man and boy circled each other. Niko aped his

master's movements and stepped evenly right-left and left-right, eyes half-slitted, fastened on Lord Amber, without blinking. A trickle of sweat dripped down Niko's forehead.

Suddenly Lord Amber advanced, thrusting his sword at Niko's face. Niko reacted automatically, pushing Lord Amber's sword away.

Lord Amber stepped back. "Good."

And then, before Niko could move, Lord Amber advanced again, his sword slicing through the dusty sunlight, coming down on top of Niko's. Niko wanted to swing upward, but instead he held his sword firm and steady so that it absorbed the blow and stuck to Lord Amber's.

"I see you understand the principle of stickiness," said Lord Amber. "Just as you hold the calligraphy pen steady in your hand, so too the sword must be held, for one wrong flick of the wrist can cause your death, just as one flick of the pen can cause an ink-blot."

As he breathed evenly, concentrating still, Niko's instinct told him this was the moment to make his move, to show Lord Amber just how ready he was to be a warrior. He turned quickly, thrusting toward the left. He backed Lord Amber into a corner between a window and a rack filled with spears.

Niko smiled. He couldn't help it. He had trapped

his master in the corner. I am already a fine warrior, he thought, just as Lord Amber dodged to the right. Lord Amber thrust his sword smoothly upward and jabbed Niko on the cheek. Niko felt the pain of the cut and the warm trickle of blood down his face.

"I could kill you right now," whispered Lord Amber in a hollow voice. "You fight well for a boy, but you made one deadly mistake. You allowed your mind to stop and I was able to make your sword my own."

Niko wiped the blood from his cheek with the sleeve of his tunic.

"Now, hand me your sword."

Niko held out the gleaming blade and Lord Amber took it, although he didn't put it away as Niko had expected. Instead, he stared at the symbol on the hilt before raising his eyes.

"Do you know whose sword this was?"

Niko shook his head. Lord Amber paused, staring at him, his dark eyes like slabs of obsidian, dark and impossible to read. Niko could see his own reflection mirrored back at him, his pale face, his expression of surprise. Lord Amber waited another moment, and Niko wondered if he had decided not to answer his own question after all.

"This sword belonged to Janus."

Niko trembled, partly with excitement and partly with fear.

"I trained Janus, just as I trained all the Dragons many, many years ago."

Niko was so shocked, his mouth dropped open, though no words came out. His mind whirled.

"I don't understand, Master."

"I never want to be responsible for nurturing that sort of obsession with power ever again," Lord Amber continued in a somber voice. "Besides Janus, there was another Dragon I trained who . . ." Lord Amber's voice trailed off for a moment. "Let's just say the two of them did each other in, just like the gingham dog and the calico cat from the old nursery rhyme, who when left to their own devices ate each other up. Then when you came, I thought it was fate giving me another chance to mold a boy into understanding the way of the peaceful warrior."

Lord Amber paused, his eyes looked searchingly into Niko's. "Remember, Niko, to fight is not the goal of a true warrior of the pen and sword. The true goal is to walk in the light and to bring everyone else safely out of the dark. Without passing through your door, you can know the way of the world. Without looking through your window, you can see the way. Thus you can know without going. See without—"

The ringing of the castle bells cut off what Lord Amber had been about to say. Niko jumped, surprised at the sound, for the castle bells rang only in times of great joy or great trouble. Seconds later, Mal appeared.

"A messenger has come from the Emperor, my lord," said Mal, unable to hide the surprise in his voice. "It seems he's taken a turn for the worse."

"The time has come and so the Chooser," murmured Lord Amber.

Before Niko could ask Lord Amber to explain what he meant, his master was gone, and the sword with him. Niko stood for a moment, alone with his falcon in the tower room, and then he turned and followed.

The hum of voices led him to the main staircase, leading down to the great hall. Niko saw Mal open the front doors and bid good-bye to the messenger. Then Lord Amber appeared, dressed in a rich royal blue cloak with a velvet hood and cuffs, the hawk crest embroidered on the back in gold. Niko had never seen Lord Amber wear such a rich cloak before. The old man said something to Mal and then left.

Niko slumped down on the steps, a strange foreboding filling him. The master never left the castle. Somehow he felt as if this departure were his fault. And he wished, for just a moment, that he had never opened the forbidden door.

But, of course, it was too late for that.

CHAPTER 2

"I wish I had a purple silk dress with a lace collar," Romany said to her best friend.

"Careful!" cried Aurora as Romany lost hold of the bucket and water spilled onto the dusty ground.

Aurora helped Romany right the bucket, smiling at her sheepish expression. Aurora always expected at least one minor mishap whenever they played "I wish." Romany became so involved in her dreams she forgot what she was doing and even where she was. The dirt and the noise of the Gypsy camp had no place in any of her fantasies.

"And matching purple shoes and a house with real glass in the windows and purple curtains and . . ."

Aurora listened without really hearing as she pushed the rusty handle of the pump. Her right hand ached, so she switched to her left, and her eye was caught again by the strange triangular mark on her palm—the sign of the Dragon's Eye. It had gotten darker lately and begun to throb, but she hadn't told her grandmother, Titi. She didn't want to think about the mark at all. Something about its strangeness and the look in Titi's eyes when she first noticed it made Aurora wish it would just go away.

"And I wish I had a maid to help me dress and fetch and carry. . . ."

As Romany babbled on, Aurora glanced around the dusty, cluttered camp, taking in the goats and the lopsided chicken coop, the ramshackle houses, the far-off silhouettes of the gamblers by the harbor, her gaze finally resting on Cappi, Romany's little brother, who was busy bouncing a red ball. Aurora knew what she would wish for, although she never would say it aloud. Then it might never happen.

She would wish for her brother, Kareem, to come back.

"I wish you would shut your face," interrupted a gruff voice.

Both girls looked up to see Bern, his eyes narrowed in a nasty expression, his big-knuckled hands loose at his sides.

"Leave us alone," said Aurora. Her hand throbbed even more.

"You wish," said Bern. "Eh, Toby?" He turned to the small, rat-faced boy who stood beside him like a shadow. The two laughed.

"Don't pay attention to them," Aurora whispered to Romany. She began to pump water once more, her back to the boys, hoping Bern and Toby would leave the Gypsy camp and go back to the farms where they lived.

At that moment Cappi began to shriek. Aurora turned to see Bern holding the red ball over the little boy's head. With a shout he tossed it to Toby, who caught it easily and threw it back.

"Come and get it!" Bern taunted, holding the ball out to Cappi.

Cappi ran toward him, his eyes wide with hope. When he was close enough to grasp the ball, Bern jerked it out of his reach.

"Jump! Maybe you'll catch it!"

Cappi jumped, but each time Bern moved the ball just over his head. Cappi's lower lip began to tremble and tears spilled down his cheeks.

"It's mine!" he wailed. "My da gave it to me."

"Your da's not here," sneered Bern. "Anyways, he stole it. 'Cause none of you Gypsies know how to earn a living. All's you know how to do is steal from honest, hardworkin' folks like us."

Aurora strode up to Bern, her fist clenched in fury. She stopped just a foot from where he stood and stared him down with her flashing green eyes.

"Give him the ball," she said.

"You gonna make me, Gypsy girl?" taunted Bern, slouching backward, a half smile on his face.

"It's okay," said Romany, casting Aurora a nervous look. "Let him have it."

"Give. Him. The. Ball," Aurora repeated.

"I don't got to listen to you," sneered Bern. "Finders, keepers, eh?"

Aurora glared up. But instead of looking at Bern, she stared at the ball, pouring all her angry feelings into the round, red shape. Her vision blurred. A familiar tingling tickled the middle of her forehead and her palm ached. The ball spun itself out of Bern's grasp and arced through the air in a slow flight. Bern's gasp of surprise was loud, although Aurora never heard it. She was intent on the ball, her eyes following its every move, until it fell gently to the ground at Cappi's feet.

The little boy clapped in delight. He took his ball and ran away.

Bern edged back. "I know what you are." He spit out the words, his eyes little slits of horror. "You're one of them that practices the dark arts and puts curses on us and on our crops. It's them green cat eyes o' yours. 'Tain't human. I hope you die."

"Yeah, I hope you die a terrible death," echoed Toby. "And they chop up your body into pieces."

The two strode off, turning back every few yards as if to make sure Aurora wasn't casting a spell on them.

"Aurora, how did you . . ." Romany could barely speak through her openmouthed amazement.

Aurora couldn't answer. She was shaking. No one had ever wished her dead before. But more than that was the power coursing through her. She'd never moved something through the air with her mind. Sometimes she could read people's minds, and once she'd moved a stick a few inches along the ground, but that was all. This surge of power felt magical—and scary.

"Romany." She tried to find the words to explain. "I was—"

Before she could finish her sentence, Marta, the biggest gossip at the Gypsy camp, came lumbering toward them, her large stomach protruding through her thin cotton dress, her chins wiggling. Aurora was glad at least that Marta hadn't seen her display with the ball, for then word would be out all over the camp and she would never hear the end of it.

"Somebody's come," said Marta, breathing heavily.

"Who?" asked Aurora.

"Somebody askin' to have 'er cards read. Somebody who don't want nobody to know she's here, because she's all in black and her face is covered up. She look rich so I tol' her I'd bring a card reader. Titi's nowhere to be found so that leaves you."

Aurora shuffled her feet for a minute. "Titi's gone to birth Tawnie's baby," she explained to Marta. "Left early this morning."

"Go on, girl," urged Marta. "Then it's up to you."

Aurora left Romany and Cappi, wondering what to do. She'd never read the cards on her own before. The one-room shack they shared was similar to the makeshift houses dotting the camp except for the flowers and plants that grew wild in front—the herbs Titi used to make medicines. Thyme for a cough and chamomile for headache and so many others. The spicy sweet smell tickled Aurora's nose as she dashed under the old woolen blanket that served as a door.

Just as Marta had said, a stranger dressed in black sat at the small round table in the center of the room. Her hood was drawn tightly around her face so that only her almond-shaped eyes and the hint of high cheekbones were visible. Aurora wondered why anyone would wear a hood in the stifling heat of the room.

"Hello," said Aurora softly. She couldn't decide whether Titi would think it was right for her to do a reading alone, since her training was only half complete. Should she tell the stranger she wasn't the real card reader, or try her hand at doing the reading by herself? Titi would certainly be glad of the money.

The stranger didn't say anything. She studied Aurora while she tapped her small foot nervously on the hard-packed earth of the floor. Aurora noticed with surprise that she was wearing soft slippers decorated with pearls and precious stones. The nervous tapping echoed in her head like a warning.

"You know, I'm not really the—" Aurora began.

"I need you to do something for me—something very important," interrupted the stranger in a soft, cultured voice, as if Aurora hadn't spoken a word. "There is very little time and no one, not a soul from the palace, must know, or . . ." Her words trailed off as her eyes darted to the window. She cocked her head, listening for something. Aurora strained her ears to hear it too but could make out nothing other than the normal afternoon sounds—bleating goats, clucking chickens, muffled laughter.

"Here," said the stranger, and she handed Aurora a flat brown parcel, tied with a thin hemp cord.

Aurora's work-roughened fingers touched the stranger's smooth white skin, and for an instant Aurora felt such fear, she almost dropped the parcel. Images flashed into her mind.

A bed draped in white linen, candles burning, an old man whispering something about the nine charms of the Lords of Time, five monkeys all in a row, white powder falling into a glass, a baby in a cradle. A man dressed in yellow silk, speaking in a voice that was soft yet menacing, like the purring of a snow lion before it pounces on its prey . . . Someone screaming and screaming . . .

"Please, deliver this as soon as possible," said the stranger, jolting Aurora back to the moment. "It is a matter of life and death, of more consequence than you can possibly know."

"Who are you?" Aurora gasped as footsteps pounded on the hard dirt. She jumped as the blanket was thrust aside and two imperial guards stepped into the room.

"We have been searching for you, Your Majesty," said the first, bowing low.

"Ambassador Le Croix was worried that you had gotten lost," added the second, also bowing.

Your Majesty, thought Aurora, her eyes widening

as the stranger suddenly loosened her cloak with one decisive movement and pulled off her hood. She was breathtaking, with high cheekbones and very fair skin. Her lilac trousers were embroidered with silver flowers, and her white silk shirt was fastened at the collar with a glittering diamond pin. Pearls were braided through her long black hair, which was gathered in a circlet of diamonds and rubies. She gleamed in the bare room like a jewel in the dirt.

"I am hardly lost," said the Empress with a toss of her shiny hair, as her lips curled in an expression of disdain. "I was simply having my cards read. And now you may escort me back to the palace."

The guards shifted and nodded, clearly uncomfortable. She turned to go, the guards behind her, and her almond eyes met Aurora's one final time, all her haughtiness gone, their pleading unmistakable. And then she was gone, a faint smell of lavender the only reminder that she had ever been there at all.

Aurora stood frozen for a moment. Had the Empress of Sunnebēam just been in her very own home? She looked down at the parcel clutched in one hand. The encounter *had* been real. She saw that the package was addressed to Lord Amber. Aurora had heard Titi and the old ones speak of him. She knew he had once been very powerful in the kingdom but now lived in virtual isolation in his castle, less than a day's walk through the forest from the Gypsy camp. She'd seen its tall gray towers once far in the distance when she'd climbed a juniper tree looking for the berries Titi used in a plaster to cure gout.

Aurora slumped in a chair, turning the parcel over and over. She ought to go and deliver it right away. It seemed to burn in her hand as she stared at the black ink—Castle of the Seven Towers. What had the Empress said, it was a matter of life and death? It would be best if she could wait for Titi to come home, but the Empress had looked so desperate, and birthing a baby could take more than a day. The more Aurora thought about it, the more she felt sure Titi would have wanted her to go. She sprang to her feet and headed for the door.

She bumped into someone just as she pushed back the blanket. Titi *was* back, just in time.

"Titi, I have to show you—" began Aurora, her voice rising.

She looked up, but instead of the round, wrinkled face of her grandmother, she found herself staring into the chiseled features of a strange silver-haired man. A black patch with a symbol of swirling circles covered one eye. The other eye, light blue with white streaks like splinters of ice, studied her coldly.

"What do you have to show me?" said the man. His soft-and-hard-at-the-same-time voice sounded familiar to Aurora, although she couldn't place it.

"Nothing," she answered truthfully, slipping the package behind her. "I was looking for my grandmother."

The man nodded, his one eye taking in the room.

"So, you're one of those Gypsy card readers, are you? A fortune-teller." He posed the question as if it were a statement requiring no reply. "How fortunate. I was just looking for someone to read my cards."

Before Aurora could protest, he pulled out a chair and sat at the table.

"I have traveled long and far to find out what lies in my future, and who better to assist me than a Gypsy? A beautiful one at that. Do not deny me, Gypsy enchantress." He bowed, a courtly gesture in such a humble room. "Castor Le Croix, ambassador to Sunnebēam from the kingdom of Kasmania, is honored to try your skill."

Aurora gulped as she stared through the curtain of long dark hair that had fallen across her face. She didn't like this strange man or the way he looked at her.

"It's my gran you want. She's the one who reads

the cards." The words came out in a small, tight voice.

He put one hand on her arm. "You strike me as a young lady with powers of her own. At the risk of repeating myself, I would be honored to have you do my reading."

He smiled, his one eye still upon her, his hand on her arm, and Aurora realized with a shiver that she had no choice. The faster she did the reading, the faster he would leave. She slid into Titi's chair, slipping the parcel to the floor beneath her seat, and began to shuffle the cards. Finally she pushed the stack toward the ambassador, trying to hide her shaking hands.

"What do you wish me to do?" asked the smooth, silky voice.

Aurora swallowed, her mouth suddenly dry. "First you shuffle them, putting everything out of your mind except the question you want answered."

"I see," said Castor Le Croix, reaching for the cards.

Aurora watched him shuffle, his long, manicured fingers with the rings glittering. "Now what?"

"Now I read them." Slowly Aurora turned over the first card. It was the Wheel of Fortune, which she carefully placed in the center of the table. The winged figure of Fortune stood in the center of a wheel with an old man in a white robe and three children ranged round her. What does the first card mean? Aurora forced herself to think, but she wasn't very good at card reading. Titi's friend Uma said she didn't have it in her blood, not like the spices and the mind tricks. And then Uma's eyes would search out Titi's, and Aurora knew they were thinking of her mother. The spices were her mother's strongest power and part of what went wrong in the end, though Aurora knew nothing more.

She shook her head to clear it of her useless thoughts. Concentrate on the card, she told herself. "This represents you," she finally said out loud. "It shows what's going on in your life."

"Yes, I see. And what would that be?"

Aurora searched her memory for anything that would get rid of Castor Le Croix and the knot of fear in her stomach. She was about to make something up when the words flowed into her mind. She knew instinctively that they were right. "All that is will end. Destiny is running its course. Everything that is happening now was meant to be from the beginning and must be allowed to unfold. Do not fight it."

She looked up and caught a flicker of surprise in

Castor Le Croix's one eye. "How poetic. Continue, please."

Aurora reached for the next card. "This shows what obstacles lie ahead of you." She turned it over and laid it on the first card, forming a cross. It was the Moon.

"And what does this mean?" The voice was light and teasing, but underneath Aurora could hear tension.

Aurora gulped. The Moon was the darkest of all the cards, worse even than the Hanged Man. She frowned. What were the cards trying to say? For she knew they never lied.

"Cat got your tongue?" Castor Le Croix purred. Aurora felt the stirring of a blurred memory.

"The Moon means false friends. Double-dealing." Her words came out in a whisper as she suddenly remembered that voice. "That's all I can see. The reading is complete." Aurora's eyes darted to the smooth, shiny silk of Castor's robe. It was the yellow silk on the man she had seen in her mind-flash, the man who frightened the Empress so much. Aurora's throat tightened as fear rose in her stomach.

"Interesting, my dear. Now, is there something else you'd like to tell me? Or show me, perhaps?" The silky voice was harsher now, insistent.

She took a deep breath and smiled dumbly at him as if she were slow and hadn't grasped what he'd said.

"You want your palms read too?"

Castor pushed back his chair and stood frowning down at her. "Enough of this charade. Give me the package."

Aurora stepped lightly to her feet, her toes touching the parcel. "What do you mean?"

Castor Le Croix moved toward her. "If you do not relinquish what I seek, you will be sorrier than you can possibly imagine."

The ambassador moved closer, his pale face just inches from her own.

"This . . . er, something of which I speak must be in this room. If you will not give it to me, then I shall have to search for it myself, and when I find it, as I most surely shall, you will be very, very sorry that you did not do the finding yourself."

With that, he grabbed her arm and pressed hard, digging his gold rings into her soft flesh. Aurora bit her lip to keep from crying out in pain.

"I don't know what you're talking about."

"I believe you do, which means you're lying to me. I don't like to be lied to."

Le Croix jerked Aurora's arm up behind her back and held it there. Tears gathered behind her eyelids.

"I will ask you once more and once more only. Where is the package the Empress left behind? You realize that she is quite out of her head and does not know what she is doing, so it is in her best interest that I take care of this matter. In the combined interests of both of our kingdoms, I might add. There are some in this land who do not trust the Empress. Some even blame her for the Emperor's illness. That is why I am here, to protect my cousin and to ensure her safety and that of her baby, the heir to the kingdom of Sunnebēam."

Castor twisted her arm once more, the pain white hot, searing through her shoulder.

"That which I seek," demanded the voice in her ear. "I will not wait much longer."

Aurora struggled to keep silent. The ambassador stood just inches from the chair where the parcel lay. She gulped, her eyes darting quickly to it. How could she have been so stupid as to leave it out in plain sight? She glanced away, her face flushing in agitation, and saw with a sickening jolt in the pit of her stomach that Castor Le Croix had followed her glance.

"Ah, what do we have here?" He turned, his hand still on Aurora's shoulder, and bent toward the parcel, pulling her down with him.

Aurora did the only thing she could think of. She

bit his soft white hand so hard that warm blood spurted between her teeth. Castor turned to her, gasping in fury.

"How dare you, you low-life Gypsy!"

But Aurora was too fast. She grabbed the parcel and ran to the door. She was about to push her way past the blanket when she felt arms around her waist, pulling her back. She kicked backward as hard as she could, catching Castor in the shins, and then she ran out the door, across the hard earth, and into the woods. The sun slipped low on the horizon and shadows covered her path.

CHAPTER 3

Late that night, Niko slept fitfully, tossing and turning, damp with sweat. Clouds scudded across the dark sky as the wind picked up, blowing the curtains. Topaz sat on the windowsill staring at the windswept water below with hooded yellow eyes. The falcon turned, ears alert, as the windy silence was broken by sound. Two sounds, really, that came again and again. Topaz flew to Niko's shoulder and pecked him on the cheek. He bolted up in bed. "What is it, girl?"

Creak. Thud. Creak. Thud. Something was out there.

Be calm, Niko thought as he slipped out of bed. *Creak. Thud.* He tiptoed over to the window and stared out. He almost fell down with relief. It was just a branch blowing in the wind against the window. *Creak. Thud.*

Niko jumped back into bed, feeling foolish. Lord Amber so rarely left the castle that his going made Niko uneasy. He wondered where his master had gone. His trip must have something to do with the opening of the box. Why else would the messenger have come, if not to summon the new regent to the Emperor's deathbed?

Niko turned on his side and raised his knees to his chest, breathing slowly and deeply. Just as he began to drift off to sleep, he awoke again. It wasn't the *creak-thud* of the branch this time but a series of thumps and rustles that seemed to be coming from the floor below. And the patter of what sounded like horses' hooves on the cobblestones of the bridge.

Good, thought Niko, the master has returned. He turned over and lay on his back, staring up at the cracks in the ceiling, but sleep would not come. He had to know if Lord Amber was truly to be the regent.

Niko slipped out of bed for the second time that night, shrugging quickly into his clothes. When he opened the door, he heard muffled voices rising from below. One of them sounded like Lord Amber, but there were others he did not recognize.

He crept out of the room, Topaz flying just ahead, weaving in and out of the strange shadows cast by the sconces high on the walls. The noise was coming from the main hall, and the voices grew louder as he approached. Someone was shouting. What was going on?

Niko made his way slowly down the tower stairs to the main hall. The front doors were open and the night breeze blowing so that he shivered. He was about to close the doors when he heard footsteps. Something wasn't right. Instinct made him duck under the stairs, into the dark, cobwebby recess where he used to hide when he was small. Topaz flew in behind him, her yellow eyes glowing in the darkness. It was probably just Mal coming to close the doors, Niko reasoned, trying to calm himself. He was about to step out and show himself when he saw a pair of black boots. In the moonlight he could see the silhouette of a helmet with feathers on top that were ruffled by the breeze. He had never seen clothes like those before.

More footsteps. Niko's heart was beating so fast, he was afraid whoever was out there would be able to hear it.

"Have you found them?" asked a deep voice.

There was a muffled reply.

"And the boy—" The deep voice was cut off by a shout from farther down the hall. The two figures ran off in the direction of the sound.

Niko didn't waste another second. He had to find Lord Amber. He raced down the hall, sticking to the shadows, until he reached the staircase to the fifth tower. He paused, but everything seemed quiet. He took the stairs two at a time.

Niko pushed open the heavy door and stepped into the familiar glow of Lord Amber's study, a place where he and Lord Amber spent hours reading, meditating, and researching mysteries of the ground and of the sky, and of other worlds too. Niko stopped in dismay. The room had been torn apart. Books were scattered all over the floor, parchment pages ripped out, the hourglass broken, desk drawers overturned, bookcases toppled.

And there was no sign of his master.

Niko heard the thumping on the stairs behind him at the same moment he spotted something shiny sticking out beneath one of the bookcases. It caught the moonlight that filtered through the leaded glass of the small tower window, gleaming silver. The sword! He ran to it as the footsteps grew louder. He grasped the handle and pulled, prying it loose just as the footsteps sounded on the stone outside the door. At least he had had the foresight to close it.

The few precious seconds that gave him were just enough to find the stone with the jagged edge in the wall, seventh from the bottom, third from the left. He pushed and the wall swung open, revealing dense blackness beyond. He stepped inside the secret passage, Topaz a blurred streak above his head, and pulled it shut just as the door of Lord Amber's study burst open.

Niko was safe, at least for now. He would have smiled if he hadn't realized in the same instant, panic rising like sickness in his stomach, that once the wall was shut it could not be opened from inside. He was all alone with his falcon in the blackness.

CHAPTER 4

The woods were dark and still; only the hoot of an owl or the swish of a bat's wings broke the silence. Aurora hurried, glancing over her shoulder every few steps, unable to shake the feeling that she was being followed. She'd been walking for hours and was farther from home than she'd ever been. But no one knew these woods as she did, she reminded herself. Tracking her would be nearly impossible. She stumbled and sprawled on the damp forest floor. "They'll find you for sure if you lose your wits. Pay attention, girl," she scolded herself.

As she scrambled to her feet, she took a deep

breath, feeling for the reassuring bulge of the package in her pouch. This was no time to be afraid. She had to deliver the parcel to Lord Amber for the Empress and for the kingdom.

She wondered for the millionth time what could be so important in the small package. It wasn't much to look at. Just plain brown paper, tied with simple, rough string. It weighed nearly nothing. She yawned, feeling the tiredness in her bones.

Aurora picked her way carefully through the dense jumble of tall, ancient trees with gnarled roots and twisted branches. A twig snapped somewhere up ahead and she jumped. It's nothing, she reminded herself. Just an animal. She concentrated on the tree before her, trying to calm herself. It was a yew, the oldest tree in the world. A magical tree that kept evil forces away. Protect me now, thought Aurora, guard me from evil. She shivered, pushing the fear away, concentrating instead on the towering oak tree she was passing. A tree of wisdom. If you burned oak branches and scattered the ashes on your crops, they would be protected from disease. She couldn't banish her fear, though. She wished Titi were with her now in the dark forest. Wished she'd waited for her to come home.

Titi would not be afraid. She would tell Aurora to embrace her fear and examine it like some strange plant she'd found in the forest. Did her fear have sharp black thorns like wormwood or round yellow berries like feverfew? And then Aurora would laugh and forget she was afraid.

But now when she tried to embrace her fear, all she saw was endless blackness.

Up ahead the trees thinned. She hurried forward to find the Castle of the Seven Towers, high on a bluff overlooking the ocean, its spires rising up to catch the moonlight. Her heart gave a little leap and she began to run through the dwindling forest toward a stone bridge that separated her from the large courtyard of the castle beyond.

Aurora's bare feet squelched in the mud as the bridge rose up before her, its old stone dark in the moonlight. The castle doors burst open. At first she thought someone had seen her and had come to greet her. But when she drew a few paces closer, her eyes widened in horror and she staggered backward into the darkness as tall black horses rode toward her. The spiked, feathered helmets of their riders cast long shadows in the glow of the orange flamethrowers they held in their hands.

Quickly Aurora climbed over the side of the bridge and lowered herself out of sight. Her fingers strained to keep hold of the old stones as fear coursed through her body. She could barely breathe.

The Dragons were back, after all this time. They'd been banished by the Emperor before she was born, and they'd only been seen in the kingdom once since then, as far as Aurora knew. When she was four years old, they had come one night and burned down the Gypsy camp. No one knew why they came or where they went afterward. They just disappeared. Remembering that night, the fires burning, the screaming and crying, she had to bite her lip so that the tears wouldn't come. It was the worst night of her life because that was when the Dragons took her brother, Kareem.

"Spread out!" shouted a gruff voice. "Somebody's out there and they got what we want, so we better find 'em or the captain'll have all our heads."

Aurora gasped as realization suddenly dawned on her. The Dragons must be after her parcel. Castor Le Croix must have sent them after her. So the Dragons must be working for him now. Could they be the reason Kasmania had violated the treaty with Sunnebēam and begun to invade some of the lands in the north? Aurora frowned, thinking of the Empress. No wonder she was so scared. Even though she was from Kasmania, she was the Empress of this kingdom now. Her loyalty was to Sunnebēam. And the Dragons were the most ferocious warriors of all time, for one terrible reason. They were not afraid to die, so they had nothing to lose.

"You two stay on the bridge and don't let anybody pass."

What was Aurora going to do now? It was one thing to escape Castor Le Croix, but to slip through a whole band of Dragons was impossible. She decided to sneak back to the woods and wait there for the Dragons to leave. She was about to climb down when she heard a sound beneath her. A figure was crawling out of an opening in the stones, his shadowy presence menacing in the moonlight.

A Dragon!

Aurora stayed as still as possible, hoping he hadn't seen her. But he never glanced up. All his attention was focused on something lying at his feet. Through squinted eyes she could just see what it was—something small and brown, tied with rope. Her parcel! She must have dropped it when she swung over the bridge to hide.

What could she do? She was just a girl. How could she battle a Dragon? The Empress's sad, pleading face flashed before her eyes. She thought of the guards and Castor's soft, cruel voice. And she knew she must try. Her fear was bitter in her mouth like rue, and she remembered suddenly that rue also guarded you from evil things.

Evil things like Dragons.

Aurora reached beneath her dress and pulled a white dagger out of the pouch she wore around her waist. The Dragon was still bent over the parcel. She could see the silver gleam of his sword. Without allowing herself another moment to reconsider, she jumped off the ledge. Her aim was good, and she landed squarely on the soldier's back, knocking the wind out of him. The two rolled on the wet ground. Sandy mud filled Aurora's nose and mouth, making it difficult to breathe, and sharp marsh grass prickled her skin, but she didn't let go. Quickly, before the Dragon broke his sword arm free, she swung her hand up and held her dagger to his throat.

"Give me that package or I'll . . . I'll . . ." She searched her mind for a suitable threat. "I'll slit your throat."

She was shaking from fear and from exertion, so much so that it took her a moment to notice that she hadn't attacked a Dragon at all, but a boy. Aurora stared at his pale face in the moonlight, the dark brown hair and silvery gray eyes. Her mouth opened and closed, but no words came out.

"Let go of me!" said Niko.

"Not until you give me my parcel." She moved the dagger closer to the boy's throat for emphasis.

"All right." Niko stared into the wild green eyes and dirt-streaked face. He dropped the package and watched her pounce on it, rubbing it against her tattered cotton dress.

Aurora felt the boy's eyes on her and blushed. "My name's Aurora. Sorry about the dagger."

"Niko," the boy grumbled.

"I have to get to the castle," she said. "And give this to Lord Amber, but with the Dragons—"

"You might as well give it to me," Niko interrupted with haughty condescension. "Because there are soldiers all over the castle and it's no place for a girl."

At that they both looked at the white dagger Aurora still held and color flooded Niko's cheeks. His fingers reached for his sword.

"Soldiers," said Aurora. "You mean Dragons, don't you?"

"Dragons?"

Aurora nodded. "Tall black horses. Feathers on their helmets. Flamethrowers, right?"

Niko frowned, thinking back on the silhouettes in the great hall. He didn't say anything for a long moment.

"I thought the Dragons were banished," he said at last, breaking the silence.

He remembered Ruah's conversation with Mal, her worried words about the Dragons and the dark one. And he knew fear. These soldiers were legendary killers. But no matter. He had to get back inside the castle, find Lord Amber, and help defend his home. He clutched the silver sword tightly.

"I have to go."

He turned awkwardly, the large sword held in one hand like a flagstaff, and headed up the bank toward the bridge.

Aurora ran after him.

"Listen, there are Dragons on the bridge. I saw them. Maybe you should go another way."

"I don't have time," said Niko, with a quick glance at the bridge. "Anyway, there's no one up there now. And it's none of your business what I do."

Aurora followed his glance. The bridge was clear. She watched the boy scale the stone wall, watched the shimmering green of his cloak billow in the night wind. He was right, too. It was none of her business what he did. She was just a Gypsy girl. She shouldn't even be here in the first place. She should have waited for Titi to come back.

She was about to give up and go home when she

noticed a shower of dirt and rocks cascading to the water below. It was Niko. He had lost his footing. She watched as he righted himself and began to climb up the side of the bridge once more. He wasn't a very good climber, she noticed. As she watched him, a flash of light caught her eye. She thought for a fleeting moment that it might be a shooting star, a soul gone up to heaven, the old ones always said. But a second glance revealed that it was a torch attached to a Dragon! Niko was just feet below him, climbing slowly up the stones of the bridge, oblivious to the danger. The Dragon turned slowly, as if he sensed Niko below.

Aurora blocked out her fears of the Dragons and the burning circles of fire they left in their wake. She pushed aside memories of the night they took Kareem when he tried to protect her from their mighty swords with his small white dagger. She shinned up the bridge, her toes moving nimbly. This was easier than climbing the trees around the camp, which offered no crevice or hold. She was just feet away. But she couldn't make a sound or the Dragon would hear, and then they would both be found out.

She reached up to pull on the leg of Niko's pants, but he was too far away for her to reach. She moved up a few more inches. Still he was too far above. When she was finally within striking range, she saw the boy's hands grasp the railing. He was about to pull himself up onto the bridge and into plain sight when Aurora stretched up her arm. Her fingers felt the smooth cotton of his pants. Safe, she thought.

"This way!" shouted another Dragon. "There's something down here."

Voices answered, Dragons running to help.

There was a crash as something hit the ground.

"Something's above us!" yelled a voice.

While the soldiers looked up, Aurora pulled with all her might and Niko fell, landing with a splash in the marsh below. She jumped after him. Luckily, the tide was coming in and the water was deep enough to cushion their fall.

Niko's pale face was angry in the gloom. "What did you do that for?"

She motioned for him to crawl with her into the shadows under the bridge. "There were Dragons. They almost saw you."

Before Niko could say anything else, Topaz landed on his shoulder in a flurry of feathers.

Aurora jumped. "That your bird?"

Niko nodded. "You know, I could have gotten into the castle if you hadn't grabbed me."

"I didn't think you knew the Dragons were up there."

"I can take care of myself."

She stepped closer, reaching out to the bird. "Sorry."

"Don't!" warned Niko. "You don't just touch a bird of prey. See that beak? It can tear a rabbit apart in seconds, and that's what it'll do to your hand if you don't watch out."

But Aurora had begun to stroke Topaz's crest feathers. "Falcon, isn't she? Maybe she'll bring you some luck. They say because of those black markings beneath their eyes that falcons are magic birds, all-seeing. Birds of the light. Hope in darkness. Something like that." Stop babbling, she told herself, but she was tired and at the edge of her nerves, and the words kept coming.

Topaz, to Niko's amazement, actually began to coo.

"What's her name?"

"Topaz," Niko answered quickly, unable to hide the surprise in his voice. "Now, I've got to find my master. I guess I'll go through the marshes. No use taking any more chances." He turned abruptly and walked up the bank toward the tall grass.

Aurora hesitated for a moment and then ran after him. She didn't know why exactly, couldn't put it into words, but she had a feeling she should. Titi had always told her to trust her feelings, her instincts, even if they didn't make sense. Certainly it was senseless for her to follow this arrogant, helpless boy into terrible danger. No matter how tough Niko thought he was, he was still just one boy against a whole army of Dragons. She couldn't let him go alone. And there was still the package for Lord Amber. She had promised to deliver it, and Aurora always kept her promises.

"Can I come with you? I have to deliver this."

"Suit yourself," said Niko, his tone not hostile but not friendly either.

They wandered around the bridge, heading for the rear of the castle, knee-deep in mud and water, hidden by the waving grass. They met no Dragons, the squelching of mud beneath their feet the only sound. Aurora turned to Niko and studied him curiously.

They said no more until the dark gates of the castle loomed before them. They waited a moment but spotted no Dragons, not even a sentry in sight. Cautiously Niko led the way into the rear courtyard through a broken slat. They stood on the flagstones, listening.

"It's too quiet," Aurora whispered.

Niko nodded. He had been thinking the same thing. He stepped carefully through the small arched door into the kitchen. They crept across the wide stone floor into the great hall, which ran the length of the castle, a vast, high-ceilinged, drafty room, dimly lit by candles in sconces high on the walls. Quickly they moved along the hall toward the front of the castle, but all was silent. Where were the servants? Niko wondered. Had Ruah and Mal fled? He held his sword before him and moved slowly toward the great staircase that led to Lord Amber's study. Aurora followed closely behind.

Something crashed to the ground and they both froze. Whoever or whatever it was lurked around the front of the stairs. They crept forward, Aurora clutching her dagger, Niko holding his sword. The sound came again and Niko moved toward it, slipping around the dark staircase. He stopped short and Aurora plowed into him. Three bodies littered the floor.

"Ruah! Mal! No. My lord, wake up," Niko cried. Aurora couldn't hold back the small scream that escaped from her throat. There was blood everywhere, and such a look of horror and surprise in the old woman's eyes that Aurora felt tears running down her cheeks. Castor sent those Dragons to find her package and those Dragons killed innocent people searching for it. Their death was her fault. If she had been faster, delivered the package sooner, maybe these people would have been spared.

Niko, meanwhile, had crouched on the floor next

to the bodies. He was holding a slashed and blood-stained blue robe with a patch on the breast pocket.

"Niko," she began.

But he didn't answer. He just stared at the robe in his hands, stroking it gently with one finger and rocking back and forth on his heels. Faraway footsteps echoed behind them in the empty hall.

"Niko." Aurora tried to rouse him as the footsteps grew louder. Someone was out there. Coming closer.

Niko didn't move. He clutched the robe in both hands.

"Niko, we have to get out of here."

Still Niko did not move. It was as if she hadn't spoken.

The footsteps kept coming. Someone was definitely moving their way, more than one Dragon, most likely. They had to get out of the castle as soon as possible or—Aurora shuddered—they'd wind up like the bodies in front of them.

Aurora bent and pulled on Niko's sleeve. He shrugged her off almost angrily.

"Niko, we have to go." Her whisper was tense and urgent.

"Leave me alone." He squeezed the words out between clenched teeth.

Aurora shifted from foot to foot, wondering how to reach this boy she barely knew. She faced Niko so that she could look into his eyes. Niko, she thought, but she did not speak aloud. Instead, she felt the familiar tingling in her palm. She breathed deeply and concentrated on Niko's eyes. She pushed her worries about the approaching Dragons to the front of her mind, gathering her fear in a powerful ball, which she bounced to Niko from her eyes to his. "Heed me," she said. But Niko's thoughts were too chaotic for her to penetrate with her own. She must know his mind to plant her message.

After a moment, the tingling grew and images popped from his mind to hers, like pictures in a book. She saw a little boy running down a stone hallway. This hallway. Throwing something up in the air that a baby falcon swooped to catch. Playing pat-a-cake on someone's lap—the woman on the stairs. Sitting in front of a stack of books with a man who spoke firmly, asking complicated questions. Having dinner with the same man at a long table. Master, Niko called him.

Lord Amber, Aurora suddenly realized, and the connection snapped. Her hand flew to her mouth in horror as she looked down once more at the robe. Muffled shouts from down the hall made her jump.

She was running out of time.

Quickly she concentrated once more on Niko, sending him the only message she thought might rouse him: Lord Amber would not want you to die . . . Your master would not want you to die . . . die . . . die . . .

Niko jerked his head up suddenly, his eyes narrowing. "What are you doing to me?"

The pounding footsteps grew louder. They both turned. In the archway, less than twenty feet away, were Dragons, staring at the opened door. They hadn't spotted the pair yet.

"Which way?" mouthed Aurora as Niko scrambled to his feet.

He led them up the dark curving stairs, down one dark hall and then another until they reached an arched door. "Go," Niko urged as footsteps echoed in their ears. The Dragons were coming.

Panting, Aurora dashed up the final steps to the top of the stairs. This door was completely shattered, wood splintered all over the stones. Niko jumped over the rubble and ran to the opposite wall. Aurora bit her lip, trying to keep back the fear. But there was only one way into the room, and she could hear the thudding footsteps coming closer. Why had Niko led them into this trap? As the door banged open below them, Niko pressed on a stone in the wall and a doorway to a secret passage swung open.

He stepped into the yawning darkness and beckoned for Aurora to follow. Topaz flew just ahead of them. The section of wall swung shut for the second time that night just as a young Dragon entered the room—a warrior not much older than Niko and Aurora who scanned the chamber intently like a hunting dog on the scent of a fox, his green cat eyes finally resting on the stone wall opposite.

CHAPTER 5

Aurora stole a glimpse at Niko as he walked beside her, staring blankly at the wall of trees ahead. She knew he must be thinking of Lord Amber, and her heart went out to him.

It was hours since their escape through the secret passage, and the sun was high in the sky. As far as she could tell, no one had followed them. Topaz darted ahead and out of sight. At least they were almost to the safety of the Gypsy camp. Aurora yawned, relieved. After all this time, Titi was sure to be back from birthing Tawnie's baby.

The trees thinned as they neared the harbor. Almost there. A shadow suddenly covered their path. She looked up, worried, but it was only Topaz, circling above their heads. She began to caw, a loud *cak-cak* that set Aurora's teeth on edge. Niko frowned, staring at her.

"That's her warning," he said softly.

Aurora's heart jumped. Warning them of what? The Dragons? But that was impossible. How could they have beaten Aurora to the camp? Unless Castor had sent two squads out at the same time. She rushed ahead and rounded the bend to her home.

The Gypsy camp was in ruins. Fires smoldered, their dull red flames licking the last of the makeshift wooden houses. Smoke filled the air in gray, billowing clouds.

Not a soul was in sight.

"Titi!" cried Aurora, running. But she stopped abruptly. Her home was gone; charred beams reached up to the sky with no roof to support. She squinted through the smoke. "Titi!"

But silence was her only answer.

She turned to Niko, her eyes filling with tears. "It's all my fault. If I hadn't run off with this package, Castor Le Croix wouldn't have made the Dragons do this." She yanked it angrily out of her pouch and stared at the thin brown shape, hating it for a moment.

"It's not your fault," said Niko slowly.

"How do you know?"

Niko shrugged. He couldn't explain how he knew, and he had been taught not to speak without absolute knowledge. That was one of the master's favorite sayings: *He who speaks does not know. He who knows does not speak.* But Aurora looked at him with such intensity that he felt compelled to share his thoughts.

"Well?" Aurora prompted impatiently.

Niko spoke slowly. "The Dragons are after more than your package. I think they were looking for something else, too. Something they thought my master had or maybe had given to me. Why else would they storm my castle? They didn't know you were coming there."

"Looking for something else—like what?"

Niko shrugged again.

"Well, I think we should see what's in here." She gestured to the package. "It might answer some of our questions. Since it's addressed to your master, you might as well open it."

She thrust it toward him. Movement on the horizon caught her eye. Had she imagined it in the glare of the sun? Niko followed her gaze. They saw the lone rider at the same time, coming toward them. As he approached, they could make out the spiked helmet and the black horse decorated with red and black insignia. The colors of the Dragons.

"Hurry," she cried. "Before he sees us."

She motioned for Niko to follow her to the woods at the other end of the camp. They heard the *clomp-clomp* of the horse's hooves as the rider came charging into the camp.

"We'll never make it," Aurora gasped, searching frantically for somewhere closer to hide. The Dragon would spot them at any moment. But there was nowhere to go, just the empty plain of burned grass and the blackened hollows that had once been homes.

They ran on, and Aurora stole a glance over her shoulder. The rider was approaching the clearing; as soon as he crested the hill, he would see them. Up ahead were the crumbling remains of an old stone well. Not much of a shelter, but it was something. Aurora and Niko ducked behind it. They crouched down and strained their ears listening, but there were no more hoofbeats.

Slowly Aurora raised her head just enough to peer over the top of the well. The Dragon stood barely a stone's throw away, red chain mail glinting in the sunlight like the scaly skin of a lizard, long sword strapped across his back, walking on bare feet that made no sound, his face tilted up to the sky so that

Aurora couldn't see it, his nose sniffing the air. He turned around in a slow circle, away from the well toward the trees beyond. Aurora held her breath, but he revolved the other way and faced the well once more. He paused for a moment, and Aurora finally got a look at his face. He was younger than she'd thought—not much more than a boy—and he had a fringe of curly blue-black hair like her own.

At that moment, the thundering of hoofbeats distracted the young Dragon. He turned and waved them back, but the one on the grandest horse disregarded his signal and beckoned the riders forward.

"Jah!" barked the captain. "Enough of your insane tracking. There is nothing here. As you can see, the first troop did a very thorough job. There is no one left."

Jah shook his head fiercely. "They are here. I feel them. They have two guardians now."

"Two?" snorted the captain. "You are losing your mind, tracker."

As the argument continued, Aurora tapped Niko on the arm. "Follow me," she whispered as she got down on all fours and began to crawl toward the woods, hoping that the well would keep them hidden from sight.

Unfortunately, at that moment Jah turned his back on the captain and looked toward the well.

"I told you there were two!"

Aurora and Niko jumped to their feet and ran for the forest. But Jah was fast and the mounted Dragons, once they spotted them, were faster still. They would be upon them any second. Niko gripped his sword, but Aurora knew that was no protection against so many.

What should we do? Aurora's mind screamed in panic. There must be something. Some way to fight those evil Dragons, who had stolen her only brother. Hatred began to eat away the fear. There *was* one thing she could try. Memories of her mother and the burning flames filled her mind. *Never forget the magic of the spices, Aurora, her mother cried, for they are more powerful than anything. Born of the sun and the moon, as old as time. Guardians. Protectors. So long as your heart is pure and your desire is true.*

Aurora stopped running. She turned to the charging Dragons, held up her arms, and concentrated on the smoldering ashes all around her, pouring her anger and her pain into the burned-out, blackened earth. Her vision blurred and her palm tingled. She thought of the hottest spice—zingiber, white-hot ginger, which burned your lips like fire. She imagined zingiber flowing from her fingertips. Searing. White hot.

A single flame danced up from the ashes.

"Aurora!" Niko cried as the Dragons galloped toward them.

That flame ignited the dry grass around it, which began to crackle, more flames rising, a barrier of fire separating her from pursuit. The horses whinnied, white-eyed, rearing in the air, hurling their riders to the ground. The other Dragons fell back, but Jah kept coming. Aurora caught a glimpse of his strange green eyes as he ran toward her. They were cold and flat, dead eyes.

He was about to make a dash over the knee-high flames when they suddenly blazed into a wall of fire. With a cry, he was forced back, as red tongues of flame licked the blue sky.

Aurora hurried after Niko, sprinting for the trees, fighting for breath. As they reached the woods, she looked back. The Dragons, even the strange one, were battling her fire. But this was no ordinary fire, for it wrought no destruction, burning only where the Dragons stood, trapping them in a circle of flames.

They had been moving through the forest for so long now, Niko had completely lost track of time.

The wild jumble of branches was so thick above their heads that it was impossible to tell whether it was day or night.

He followed close behind Aurora, who had been walking randomly, he thought, moving from right to left and right again, over no path that he could see. But she seemed to know her way. Niko didn't like forests. He never had, even as a small boy on walks with Lord Amber, or tagging after Mal when he went hunting. Every creak of a branch or rustle of an animal made him jump. You never knew what was out there hiding in the trees.

Niko preferred wide-open spaces, like the sea. Or cliff tops. Or meadows. Places where you could see all around you. And if trouble was coming, you could look it square in the eye and fight back.

Aurora stopped walking and sat on an old log. She pulled a small glass vial out of the pouch beneath her dress. It was filled with some kind of dark liquid.

"Here," she said. "This'll help."

"What is it?"

"It's a Gypsy remedy that's good for the blood. It doesn't taste like much, but it'll give you some strength. My grandmother used to make it." Her voice cracked then, and she looked down to hide her tears.

"I'm sorry about your grandmother," said Niko, taking a sip of the strange brown drink. He frowned at the bitter taste.

Aurora smiled through her tears. "It's the marigold petals that make it so bitter. But they open the heart. That's why it's good for the blood."

"I see," said Niko, handing the vial back to her.

She took a sip. "I'm sorry about Lord Amber."

Niko nodded.

"How long did you live there?"

"Ever since I can remember. Someone left me on the doorstep of the castle when I was a baby and Lord Amber took me in."

"That's how it was for me with Titi. I never knew my father, and my mother died when I was young. I hardly remember her—except for her voice. She used to sing me to sleep, and she had this beautiful white lace veil she used to wear sometimes. They buried it with her." Aurora shrugged.

Both fell silent, thinking their own thoughts, listening to the birds twittering in the trees.

"It's strange, isn't it?" said Niko after a few minutes. "Neither of us really knew our parents."

Aurora nodded. "We better get moving again. It'll be dark soon. Truly dark."

They walked on through the forest. Niko replayed his sword fight with Lord Amber over and over. He wished he'd been able to apologize for disobeying, but his master had left the castle so suddenly, and then . . . Niko shook his head, an image of the slashed blue robe popping into his mind. He closed his eyes and tried to blink it away, but when he opened them again he could see it still imprinted on his mind like a sunspot.

He peered up ahead for the now familiar blue-and-yellow pattern of Aurora's dress. He decided it had probably once been pretty flowers, but it had faded so much, he couldn't be sure. How had she slipped from his sight so quickly? He shivered. He couldn't see her—or Topaz—anywhere.

Be calm, he reminded himself, clutching his sword. She's probably beyond that next tree. But she wasn't. Nor was she beyond the next or the one after that. The forest, which had seemed dark to Niko before, grew impenetrable as time passed.

"Sun must be down," he told himself.

He moved slowly, straining to hear any sounds.

Without Aurora, he shuddered to think what might have happened. That fire had saved them from sure capture and maybe death. And it had to have been her doing. Clearly, she had strange powers.

So where was she? He came to a clearing where

the forest floor was littered with damp, decaying leaves. The whole place had an earthy, musty smell, which Niko associated with death.

"Aurora!" he called.

There was no answer. Just the wind sighing in the trees.

"Aurora!" he called again, more loudly, his voice cracking, betraying his fear.

He could hear leaves moving behind him, and a branch snapped. He whipped around, pulling out his sword.

"It's only me," Aurora said, sliding down the trunk of a tree. She smoothed her dress, a small smile tugging on the corners of her lips. Topaz flew down and landed on a tree between them.

"How was I to know that?" The words came out with more bite than he had intended, but he didn't want her to think for even a moment that he had been scared.

"Listen," she continued eagerly, as if he hadn't spoken. "I climbed the tree to check for Dragons. I didn't see any, by the way. And I was trying to figure out where we are because I've never been so far in these woods before. I spotted a stream not too far from here. Less than a mile, I'd say, going northeast in the direction of the River of the Black Pearl.

We can get some water to drink. Aren't you thirsty?"

Niko nodded, his tongue cleaving to the roof of his mouth. He'd been thirsty for so long, he had almost forgotten. He could practically taste the water already, sweet and cold.

They began to walk once more. Occasionally Aurora would glance up at the sky, at the pinpricks of moonlight visible here and there through the canopy of leaves. Then she would shift their course ever so slightly as if she had a wind rose such as sailors used to chart their course across the sea.

"How do you know which way we're going?" he asked after she swerved to the right past a strand of tall evergreens.

"The stars," she said, stopping and pointing. "See right there, those seven stars jutting out over that crooked branch? Some call them the Seven Brothers or the Seven Wise Men. Others say they're part of the Bear. See, over there's his tail. Anyway, if you look from those two bright stars in a straight line, that'll take you to the polestar so you know which way is north. Then east is to the right, so northeast is somewhere between."

"Oh." Niko had studied constellations in books, but he had never looked at the stars in this practical way before. This wild girl seemed to know so much that he did not, even though he'd wager she'd never cracked a book in her life.

Sometime later, they reached the stream. It cut through a clearing that was barely a break in the trees.

"At least there's space enough to turn around without bumping into branches," said Aurora.

They threw themselves down and began gulping water, their motions making the water ripple in the moonlight in larger and larger concentric circles.

Aurora finished first and sat back on her heels, watching Niko drink.

"So, what do you think that Dragon meant when he said, 'They have two guardians now'? Was he talking about us? And what are we guarding?"

"I don't know. Maybe what's in the parcel," said Niko. "Let's open it now."

Aurora took the parcel out of her pouch and handed it solemnly to Niko. He ripped it open quickly, making sure not to look at the writing on the front. He couldn't think about Lord Amber anymore because he might cry. And he didn't want to cry in front of anybody, especially not a girl. Inside was a single piece of folded parchment. He pulled it out and spread it open.

"What is it?" asked Aurora, peering over his shoulder.

"Some kind of map, I think."

"Of what?"

"It's too dark to tell. We'll have to make a fire if we want to read it properly."

"What could be so life-and-death important about a map?"

Niko shrugged.

"Maybe it's the directions to something really valuable that the Emperor hid," suggested Aurora. "Or maybe it shows the way to some lost kingdom."

"We'll have to see," Niko said practically.

Aurora removed her dagger from the pouch beneath her dress and began to cut slivers of bark for the fire. "That'll take forever," Niko said after watching her slow progress. "Step aside, Aurora. I'll take care of this."

"By all means," Aurora humphed. "If you want to make a fire, that's fine with me. Good luck."

Niko looked around and spotted a branch that seemed perfect for his purpose—just within reach and big enough for a roaring blaze. He held the sword in both hands and swung with all his might. But never having chopped wood before even with an ax, he wasn't prepared for the resistance. The sword flew out of his hand, bounced off a rock, and hit the ground. The branch remained where it was, with barely a nick in it.

Aurora laughed as Niko whirled around in confusion. "I didn't think you were a woodsman," she said, and laughed again.

Niko bent to gather up his sword, mustering what little dignity he could. He saw with alarm that the hilt seemed broken—the bottom had fallen off. "Aurora, look at this." The tip of the hilt had actually swung open on a hinge, revealing a compartment.

"There's something in there," Aurora said.

Niko turned the sword upside down and shook it. Something fell onto the ground. Niko picked it up and brought it to the fire, which Aurora had managed to start from bark and twigs and a fire stone she pulled from her pouch.

In the glow of the flames, they saw that he held a purple velvet pouch.

"What is it?" asked Aurora.

Slowly Niko untied the top of the bag and turned it over. A handful of gleaming squares tumbled into his hand. Each piece was made of a strange metal, not gold and not silver but a glowing combination of both. In the center of each was a precious stone of a different color—blood red, sky blue, sun yellow, forest green, bruise violet, sunrise pink, night black, crystal clear, amethyst purple—the colors melded like a rainbow and gleamed with a brilliant light even in the dark. Niko and Aurora stared in awe at the lovely colors pulsing like heartbeats.

"What are they?" Aurora asked finally.

"I don't know," said Niko. "But I wonder if they're what the Dragons are after."

Aurora put out her finger to touch one.

"Nine," Niko counted aloud.

Nine, nine, nine, Aurora thought. Why did it seem so familiar? Nine . . .

"Nine muses," murmured Niko, thinking back on his philosophical studies with Lord Amber. "Nine, the last in a series of numbers, therefore the beginning of something else."

Aurora looked at him blankly, and suddenly her eyes widened. "The Empress. In her mind I saw an old man, whispering. He must have been the Emperor. He kept repeating the same thing over and over."

"What?

"The nine charms of the Lords of Time!"

"Nine charms," repeated Niko, confused.

"Don't you remember?" Aurora's voice rose with excitement. "*Nine charms of light.* No, that's not right. *Silver and gold.* No, that's not right either."

"What are you talking about?"

"Don't you know the nursery rhyme? Let me think."

Aurora twirled one dark curl around her finger, casting her mind back. A memory of Titi singing came to her, as they turned the earth with their hands, making a spice garden. She was little, and Kareem was there too. They all sang the words together.

> *"Nine were the charms,*
> *golden-silver, made of light,*
> *forged by the Lords of Time*
> *to help take back the night."*

Niko nodded at Aurora's recitation. Ruah used to sing the rhyme as she rocked him to sleep. He hadn't thought of the words in ages, but in a rush they all came back. He and Aurora sang the words together, filling in spaces when the other forgot.

> *"Each of these nine lords*
> *one color charm did hold,*
> *to fight the darkness rising,*
> *or so the story's told.*
>
> *But long ago the nine were lost,*
> *the Lords of Time all passed.*

Dark and light made an uneasy truce,
but never would that last.
One must find the nine,
one must have the power,
and one must come from somewhere else
to fight the Dark Lord's hour.

Silver will be his sword,
silver like his eyes.
The choosing of the charms
is where his skill lies.
Called by all the Chooser,
the charms will find his hands
to bring forth new lords of time,
strangers from strange lands.

Sign of the Dragon's Eye,
great will be the sight.
The Chooser and the charms
must be protected for the light.
Called by all the Protector,
the dreams will set all free
from what is and from what was
to what was always meant to be.

From another world
where magic is no more,
his task shall be to fight

for the light in the coming war.
Called by all the Bearer,
with his faith and derring-do
the nine doors will be opened
and the dark be vanquished too."

"You're the Chooser, aren't you?" breathed Aurora. "I mean, you've got silvery eyes and a silver sword."

Niko thought back to the last time he had seen his master. "The time has come and so the Chooser," Lord Amber had said. How could he have known?

"Niko, look." Aurora was holding up her hand. On her palm, the dark triangular sign stood out clearly in the firelight.

"The Dragon's Eye," murmured Niko, his voice rising. "That means you're the Protector, doesn't it? How could a girl protect anybody?"

"Ex*cuse* me," said Aurora, "but who saved you from the Dragon on the bridge?"

"You didn't have to, you know. I mean, I would have seen him and then hidden myself."

"Right," said Aurora, her green eyes blazing. "And what about that crazy Dragon named Jah? What were *you* going to do?" She stopped herself, lowering her eyes. "I didn't mean to say that."

Niko sighed. Whether he wanted to admit it now

or not, she *had* been protecting him ever since he'd met her. Still, it was absurd, wasn't it? A girl couldn't protect him. And for that matter, how could *he* be someone from a nursery rhyme?

"Even if you're right about those times," said Niko slowly, "that doesn't mean you have to protect me now. I am a warrior in training, you know."

"Fine," said Aurora.

"Anyway, the nine charms are just a nursery rhyme, aren't they?" Niko asked.

"I always thought so," Aurora whispered.

But there were the charms, very real before them. Niko's eyes strayed from the glowing charms to the wrinkled parchment lying on the other side of the fire, forgotten in their discovery of the pouch in the sword.

"The map," said Niko, reaching for it. "I wonder if it's got anything to do with the charms."

He smoothed out the parchment. If it was a map, it was the strangest one he'd ever seen. Much of the page was damaged from their tumble in the marsh. At the top were the words *Doors of the Hunab Ku, The Pathway to the Sky*. At the bottom were mountains with a city rising out of them, with levels marked, and decorated with strange symbols and patterns. He could make out a black horse next to a rectangle that could be a door. And something else that looked like a fish, or was it a snake? Aurora pointed to the charms. Niko wasn't surprised to see that the charms bore the same symbols as those on the map.

"Not a treasure map, is it?" she asked.

Niko shook his head. "Not as far as I can tell." He turned the map over and on the back saw a note, only part of which was readable:

To my most trusted friend,

. . . the dark one by name . . . give the map of the Doors of the Hunab Ku . . . send the . . . keeper of the Nine Charms . . . new Lords of Time . . . new regent . . . please guard . . . your name in . . . the dark . . . rising, as once you warned . . . send the . . . and summon . . . the box. I beseech you.

It was signed with the Emperor's seal. Niko tried to decipher the missing words, but the message made no sense to him. What were the Doors of the Hunab Ku? And where did they lead? And what did they have to do with the charms and the dark one?

"What's the box?" asked Aurora.

"It's the place where the Emperor puts the name

of the one he's named regent, to rule until the baby comes of age."

"So, that was supposed to be your master?"

Niko nodded.

"I should go see the Empress," said Niko slowly. "Since my master is . . . can't be the regent. It's up to me to tell her what happened and to bring her the charms."

"I'll go with you. I mean, she did give the map to me, remember? I think you should do something first, though."

"What?"

"Choose."

"What are you talking about?"

"I think you should choose the first charm, like the rhyme says."

Niko didn't answer her.

Aurora picked up the map. " 'The dark rising, send the blank . . . new Lords of Time,' " she read aloud. She looked at Niko. "I bet that means, send the charms out for a new Lord of Time."

"I don't know."

"Well, you're the Chooser—isn't choosing what you're supposed to do? Choose a charm and then send it out to bring forth a new Lord of Time? It seems to be what the Emperor wanted Lord Amber to do. And it's what the rhyme says. Then he can take care of the Dragons and you and I can go back to . . . Well, we can try to start over again."

"I don't know how to choose."

"You must, if you're the Chooser."

Niko thought of his master's face on that last day and how he had commanded Niko to choose a sword. *Choose*. The same word.

"Well?" Aurora's green eyes glowed with impatience—or was it excitement?—in the darkness.

Hesitantly Niko told her about choosing the sword; he felt his face flush, self-conscious at finding himself telling someone about something so private. He wasn't used to talking so much.

"So, choose a charm the way you chose the sword."

"I didn't choose the sword," Niko blurted out, remembering the way the light had glinted off the silver sword, drawing his eye to it. "It—this probably sounds crazy—but it chose me."

"So, that's how you choose a charm, I bet. Let it choose you."

"But I don't—" Niko began.

"It's kind of like the cards," interrupted Aurora. "Titi always has her customers shuffle them after she does. She says that way some of their spirit gets into them before they choose the two that will be their fortune. Why don't you do that?"

Niko frowned, finding her logic odd. He didn't believe in the transference of spirit into matter, but for lack of a better idea, he did as she suggested. He touched the charms one by one, turning them over so that their gemstone sides were facing up. The colors all glowed and glittered in the firelight. But one seemed to glow a little brighter, a little hotter. Niko kept finding his gaze straying to it.

Finally he picked it up and held it out to Aurora. "Now what?" The red stone caught the light and gleamed as if it had a fire inside it.

Aurora held it in her palm and began to chant. The ancient words formed themselves in her mind and rolled off her tongue. The heart chant, the old ones called it. The chant of the beginning and of the end. Of creation and destruction. Of the endless transformation of life. Her voice rose and fell, borne by the wind into the darkness of the night. Niko listened intently to the strange melody and felt the hair on the back of his neck begin to rise. Could this Gypsy truly be the Protector?

Aurora's hand twitched, and to her horror, she dropped the charm into the water.

"No!" she gasped, plunging her arm into the stream to grab it.

"What happened? Why'd you do that?"

"It got so hot, like I was holding fire. It burned so I couldn't hold it anymore and I had to let go. I didn't mean to. I don't know why I started chanting like that. I couldn't help it," she finished lamely.

"We'd better find that charm," said Niko.

"We will. The water's not very deep and I dropped it straight down."

But they did not find the charm. They looked and looked, searching every inch of the muddy stream, but the red charm was nowhere.

"I can't believe you did that," said Niko, sitting back exhausted, not hiding the anger in his tone.

"I didn't do it on purpose," answered Aurora, close to tears. "It's your fault for choosing the one with the red stone. It probably was some kind of fire stone, and that's why it burned."

"Right," said Niko. "It was your idea to choose a charm in the first place."

"Well, that's what the note said to do."

"So?"

"So, if everything was up to you, we'd both be dead." Aurora clapped her hand over her mouth. "I didn't mean—"

But the words hung in the air between them. *I'll show you,* Niko thought. *I don't need a protector. I don't need anybody.* But all he said was, "It's okay.

It wasn't your fault. It wasn't anybody's fault. We're just upset, that's all."

They both sighed and got up to search for the charm once more. But they couldn't find it anywhere.

CHAPTER 6

After the roaring water passed, there came a rushing wind—and the loudest silence Walker Crane had ever heard. He couldn't even hear himself breathe. Falling endlessly was one thing, but the silence of his own breath was really scary because without that, how did he know he was still alive?

After what felt like forever but might have been no time at all, Walker heard the whoosh of air once more as he breathed in and out. He was lying on something hard and cold, and he realized his eyes were closed. He opened them and true panic set in.

The darkness did not disappear. Impenetrable blackness, so thick that he couldn't even see his hand in front of him, threatened to suffocate him. He took a deep breath, closed his eyes, and opened them again, but it made no difference. He could see nothing.

Was he dead? Had the lightning that grazed him at the fountain killed him? He took another deep breath and tried to calm himself. You're not being logical Crane, he told himself. Of course you're not dead. You're thinking, aren't you? What was that stupid thing we learned in English last year? I think, therefore I am. Well, I'm thinking, so therefore I am, right?

"Hello," he said aloud, testing his voice, which sounded just like him, a bit fainter than usual maybe, but his voice all the same. Another reason not to think he was dead. If only he could figure out where he was. Every problem has a solution, just like in math, Walker thought.

The trick was to find it.

Slowly he lifted himself up from the hard floor. "Relax, Walker," he said softly. "You just fell under the fountain into some kind of storage closet. Or maybe it's a trapdoor so the museum can collect all the pennies in the fountain. You'll find a way out."

He stretched out his hands. Nothing but empty space. He reached behind him, hoping to encounter something solid, but again felt nothing. He crawled forward, or what he thought was forward, on his hands and knees, feeling the reassuring solidity of stone beneath him.

"Keep moving and you're bound to hit something."

But he wasn't sure whether he was going anywhere or merely traveling in circles. He crawled for hours, or maybe minutes—he couldn't tell. Time had that strange way of moving fast when you were having fun and crawling along when you were doing something you hated—or that terrified you.

Abruptly Walker slammed into a wall. He moved his hands along the smooth surface until he found a corner at his right. With his fingertips he felt the texture of the wall change. It was no longer cold and smooth, but rough and warm. He recognized the feeling, but in the dark, he couldn't remember what it was. Had he lost his mind in the fall?

"It's just a panic attack," he told himself, "like Mom got when we were in London and we rode the Underground." Walker began to breathe deeply the way she had done when the train stopped in the tunnel and the lights went out. "Calm down. One thought at a time."

He rubbed his hand over the rough surface again and something pricked him. Wood! He laughed out loud. He reached farther down and his fingers touched metal. It was some kind of latch, an old-fashioned doorknob. If he could figure out how to open the door, he could get out of the room and back to his class.

He moved his hand along the wood from left to right until he felt the stone again, and then up and down. He figured the door measured about two feet by two feet. It was small, but big enough for him to fit through. He reached for the metal latch, hoping it wasn't locked.

It wasn't.

He lifted the latch slowly and pushed. The door creaked open on its rusty hinges. "They sure don't keep up the maintenance down here," Walker murmured.

The wavering golden glow of candlelight cut the darkness. As Walker's eyes adjusted to the light, he made out the silhouette of hanging clothes. This wasn't the kind of chamber he had expected to find under a fountain. It was a closet of some sort. And he could smell a strange scent, almost like perfume but sweeter and heavier, more like the stuff they used at churches. Incense, that was it. He lifted himself through the opening. His face brushed against silky fabrics. They were robes. Red silk robes.

There was another door opposite, larger than the one he'd come through. And it was through that door that the light was slipping in.

Walker opened that door and stepped into a bare stone room, with vaulted ceilings and a small arched window. Must be an old part of the museum, he thought. He noticed there was a gold washstand with a scrollwork mirror above it, flanked by two candles on the walls. As much as he wanted to believe he had fallen into a chamber under the fountain and that he'd just walked into some kind of museum display, he somehow knew it wasn't so. Which meant only one thing. This had to be a dream. A long, bad dream.

He stepped up to the mirror. He still looked the same, same short blond hair, same blue eyes and yellow Lakers T-shirt. He looked hard at himself, letting his eyes meet the eyes in the mirror.

"Yeah, I'm looking at you," he said out loud. "That's right, I'm talking to you and I want you to listen to me real good."

He paused for a moment.

"On the count of three, I want you to wake up and forget about this whole thing. It's just a nightmare. Ready?

"One . . . two . . . three."

But the room around him didn't disappear. This was no dream. His middle finger throbbed from the splinter he'd picked up from the wooden door.

And you didn't get splinters in a dream.

Walker heard footsteps, and his eyes widened as the doorknob began to turn. Some instinct warned him to hide; he darted back into the closet and pulled the door shut behind him, just in time. Through the crack in the door, he saw a man dressed in a red robe go to the basin and wash his hands. A silvery green light flickered around him.

"Why have you come?" demanded the deep voice of the figure in the red robe.

Walker's stomach did a sickening flip-flop. How did the man know he was there? He must have seen him jump into the closet. There was no use hiding from him, then. Anyway, he hadn't done anything wrong. Walker was reaching to open the closet door when suddenly the man spoke again.

"Why have you honored me with a visit to the House of the Black Rock, Ijada, eldest Sister of the Kuxan-Sunn?"

So the red-robed man *didn't* know he was there. Then who was he talking to? As far as Walker could tell, there was no one else in the room.

"I have come to ssspeak to you of two mattersss, Your Lordship," hissed a disembodied voice that made the hairs on the back of Walker's neck prickle. "Did I not promise to be your eyes and your ears?"

"Speak, then." The lord turned, and for the first time Walker could see his face. He had dark hair cut short and strong features, a long sharp nose and a pointed jaw, but what struck Walker most was his eyes. They were so dark that the iris blended with the pupil into two black holes, empty like tunnels. Walker looked away from those eyes. If he stared into them too long he'd be drawn into their darkness.

"Word is ssspreading that the dark one isss not dead," hissed Ijada in a whispering voice, which sounded almost like the wind.

"So?" countered the lord in a flat, cold tone.

"So your sssecret isss no longer sssafe. There is nothing the Sisters can do to protect you anymore. The minds of the old ones cannot be changed. The Gypsies have long been able to know any truth."

The lord shrugged as if the information meant nothing to him. Walker shrugged too. He had no clue what all this mumbo jumbo was about.

"The second matter, Ijada?"

What kind of name is Ijada, anyway? wondered Walker.

"The first of the nine charms has been sssent out," said Ijada in her windy voice.

"A charm has been sent?" repeated the lord with sudden anger. "How is that possible? Do not the Sisters of the Kuxan-Sunn still control the pathways and the nine doors between the worlds?"

"Yesss, of course, but as you know, we do not control the dark. Or the light."

Walker heard a rustling sound as the lord moved out of view. Ijada spoke once more.

"The first charm has been sent to sssummon the first Lord of Time. The arrival of the Bearer makesss the great war inevitable. The dark and the light mussst break their uneasy truce of night and day to war again."

Charm? Walker thought.

"Which charm has been sent?" asked the lord, his voice reverberating with such force, the stone walls seemed to vibrate.

"The charm of fire and blood."

"Of course the light would choose the red charm," murmured the lord. "For it denotes the spoils of war. Have they forgotten that it also means bloodshed?"

A red charm, Walker thought. He reached into his pocket and his fingers touched the smooth, cold shape he had taken from the fountain. He pulled it out, and there in the half-light, the red stone glowed with a fiery brilliance.

Did *he* have the charm of fire and blood?

"Where is the charm now?" demanded the lord's stone-vibrating voice, setting Walker's teeth on edge.

"That I cannot tell you. The Sisters can only sssee the paths of the past and the future. The present hides her secrets from us."

"What do you see in the future?"

"I sssee the rivers turned red with blood. I sssee a red moon rising, full and round. And I sssee a door opening."

"Into what?"

"Another world."

"So the Bearer is from another world?"

"He is."

The room was silent until a knock on the door caused the silvery green light to fade.

"Your Lordship, the legions have returned," said a gruff voice.

"Come in, General," barked the lord.

A squat, bald man entered the room.

"Did they find the boy?"

What boy? wondered Walker. Are they talking about me?

The general shook his head. "They searched the castle and the grounds, with no luck. But they are still searching. Our best tracker is on his trail. He will not fail."

So they don't mean me, do they? thought Walker. He'd never been to a castle. He had to get out of here. The general left, but the lord remained, standing so that Walker could see his face once more.

"The boy will be found," murmured the lord, staring right at Walker with those black, empty eyes. "And the dark will rise again."

CHAPTER 7

Niko and Aurora slept side by side beneath a willow tree. Between them lay the silver sword, its secret compartment now holding only eight of the nine charms.

Aurora moaned softly in her sleep.

Someone was coming. Someone who slipped silently through the forest, swift yet unhurried, unnoticed like the shadows of the trees. Coming closer and closer.

She tried to sit up, but her body refused to respond. She couldn't move, but she felt the darkness of the shadow reaching toward her and the charms.

Niko! She thought the word but could not speak.

Niko! She tried again, but there was no sound. Just the quiet breathing of the shadow creeping toward them, a hunter in search of its prey.

The Chooser, the Protector, and the charms.

She saw, without wanting to see, the red chain mail that shimmered in the moonlight, like a snake's skin, slithering and sliding ever toward them. And she understood too that he would find them. His certainty was stronger than her will to stay hidden.

It's just a dream, she told herself. Just a dream.

She moaned once more and managed to break the dream spell. Her eyes snapped open and she looked around the clearing, which was beginning to glow in the early rays of the rising sun. She was confused for a moment about where she was; then Topaz flew down from the tree above and landed at her feet.

It was not a dream. The Dragon named Jah was out there, coming for them. And for the nine charms, now only eight.

"Niko!" she whispered, and softly touched his shoulder. She had been taught by the old ones to wake someone gently from a deep sleep, so that she didn't scare his soul away.

He turned, clutching his sword in one hand, but did not awaken. She shook him gently but firmly. "Niko."

His eyes opened, clouded with sleep, staring up at her in confusion.

"We have to go. The Dragon is coming."

Niko blinked and sat up. "Did you see him?"

Aurora shook her head, motioning for him to hurry. He scrambled to his feet, straining his ears. He heard nothing, but he couldn't read people's minds or make fires out of ashes either, so he didn't question her.

Niko thought for sure Aurora would lead them back into the forest on the same kind of snakelike course she'd followed before. But instead she waded out into the middle of the stream where the water came up past her knees. So she is losing our scent in water, Niko thought, the way foxes do to escape pursuing dogs.

Niko followed, shivering as the cold water drenched his thin cotton pants. The rocky bottom was hard to walk on. Something long and slimy slithered about his ankles. It's only reeds, he told himself. Water plants. He tried not to think about what else might be living in the dark water.

He slipped suddenly, sliding over the slimy rocks. He caught himself just before he fell, but he lost one of his sandals in the muddy bottom.

"Are you all right?" Aurora asked from ahead.

He looked up, felt himself flushing, and kicked off the other sandal. "Fine. Just keep going. You don't have to worry about me." His tone was biting and Aurora only grunted in reply.

It was well and good for her to be the Protector, Niko thought, but he was a warrior in training and he could take care of himself. She was the one who had lost the charm, not him. What kind of protection was that?

They continued trudging through the icy water. "I wish I could fly with you, girl," Niko whispered to Topaz, circling above their heads.

A crackling like snapping branches brought Niko and Aurora to a stop. They turned and stared at each other. Aurora looked away first, her bright eyes searching the darkness for Jah. But she saw nothing, just trees, water, stars, more trees, Niko's still silhouette in the early-morning sun. And then they heard a thin screeching and the flapping of wings.

It was just a hawk catching its prey.

Aurora started moving once more, leading the way through the freezing water, trying not to think about her dream that was more than a dream. About the Dragon who had managed to find them after all her dodging and doubling back, twisting and turning through the forest. She'd never heard of a better tracker. True panic gripped her so strongly, it nearly took her breath away.

She would never tell Niko, but she didn't know how they could escape this Dragon, whose eyes were keener than an owl's and whose nose was sharper than a wolf's. He was more than just a soldier. This Dragon had power.

A sound that was faint at first, just the rustle of an animal through the leaves, caught her attention. She brushed the sound aside, but then she heard it again. The same rustle from the left bank of the river.

She stopped and the rustling stopped too.

Niko caught up to her and she motioned him toward the opposite bank. They reached it at the same moment, scrambling in the mud. And then she led them into the forest, hoping to lose whoever was out there in the trees. Hoping it wasn't Jah. Knowing it could be no other.

They hurried through the darkness of the tree cover. A branch snapped and Aurora jumped. But it was only Niko a few yards behind, struggling to catch up. She slowed her pace for a moment, looking back, and Niko motioned her forward, an annoyed look on his pale face, his lips tight in a leave-me-alone expression. Aurora got the hint. She knew his thoughts without entering his mind, they were so clear. So Niko has mad because she was leading. What did he need a protector for? She was just a girl. A Gypsy girl who had lost one of the charms. Niko's anger, coupled with the danger they were in, made her move faster again, forcing her way through the vines and dense undergrowth, deeper and deeper into the unfamiliar forest—and away from Niko.

A sudden thud stopped her short. She turned, looking for Niko, her heart beating faster.

He wasn't there.

He must have lagged behind. That was all. She turned and began to walk back the way she had come, slipping soundlessly between the trees.

But that noise. It had been the sound of something falling. A body. She knew that. Jah was out there, near now. Very near. And he had Niko. How could she have been so stupid as to let Niko and the charms get so far behind her?

Too late for that now. Too late.

She felt his presence before she saw him. Peering into the darkness, she saw a flash of red. And then a face, white between the trees.

It disappeared before she knew whether she had been seen.

She stood in the shadows, unmoving, the darkness of tree cover pressing on her eyeballs, wishing she could see more clearly. See Jah, who had slipped away and could be about to spring on her at this very moment.

She took a deep breath, scanning the woods, and she spotted a dark shape crumpled at the base of a tree just yards away. The glint of something silver next to it flashed in the moonlight. Niko! She hoped he wasn't dead. But where was Jah?

The answer came seconds later. Jah appeared as if made of darkness itself, a shadow crouching over Niko, who moaned. At least he was alive. Aurora watched as Jah searched through Niko's clothes. But the charms were hidden. Surely he would not find the secret compartment. Unless he had the sight too. Sight of the strongest sort, like the old ones.

But his powers could not be that great, could they?

She held her breath as he reached across Niko and picked up the sword. He studied it in the moonlight, turning it this way and that. Put it down, Aurora chanted in her mind. Put it down.

But Jah did not. Instead, he ran his fingers along the hilt.

There was not a moment to lose. Silently, Aurora slipped to the next tree, hoping he would not catch sight of her. Just one tree closer and she could make her move.

Aurora shinned up the next tree silently and hung

poised in the branches above Jah's head. Then she closed her eyes and began to breathe the way the old ones had taught her, air in one nostril and out the other. I will control you, she thought at the Dragon. I will enter your mind and confuse you. You will not find the secret compartment that holds the charms.

Her eyes widened in surprise. He was trying to enter her mind! She could feel his presence, searching for a way in, trying to locate her. She concentrated as hard as she could to stop the probing. This Dragon's powers were very strong.

Aurora pulled her mind from his, hiding her thoughts, forcing a fog to cloud her brain. She could not let him know about the sword's secret compartment.

From below, she heard Niko moan again. She watched in horror as Jah banged the sword on the ground and the secret compartment flipped open, revealing the bag of charms. She reached into her dress and felt for her dagger. She edged herself farther out on the branch and when Jah reached for the pouch, she jumped. She landed on top of him, forcing him to the ground, but he was agile and flipped her onto her back. He dropped the charms in their struggle and the pouch lay on the grass beside them.

She stared at the purple velvet as he jerked her

roughly by the collar, choking her. If she could just get the charms. Jah followed her glance and stretched his right arm across her.

"Is this what you want?" he taunted.

And in that moment, as Aurora stared at the smooth white skin of his wrist where it showed between the sleeve of his chain mail and the metal glove, she saw her chance.

With all her strength she jabbed the white dagger into the soft skin of his wrist.

Red blood stained the whiteness of Jah's skin, and he cried out in surprise, dropping the pouch. But he recovered quickly and with lightning reflexes knocked her arm so hard the dagger flew up in the air. Aurora scrambled to her feet, ready to battle on with her teeth if she must.

But Jah stopped fighting. Instead, he reached for her dagger. He turned the handle over and over, the ivory glowing white as milk in the sunlight.

A token of Aurora's memories.

"Aurora!" cried Niko.

He jumped up beside her, grabbing the pouch in one hand and wielding the sword with the other.

Aurora stared at the Dragon holding her brother's dagger, her mother's gift to Kareem before she died. And all Aurora had left of him since he was taken away. She hated to lose it.

Wordlessly she turned and darted into the woods, in the opposite direction from where they had come. Niko followed close behind. They ran as fast as they could through the dense tangle of trees, in an all-out effort to put as much distance between themselves and Jah as possible.

It was a question of time and speed—and luck. Aurora hoped fate was on their side. She couldn't get the image of the Dragon out of her mind, the way he had stroked the dagger, which had held him as if hypnotized.

And that only made her run faster. A Dragon with his powers who was also mad would be capable of anything. Anything at all.

They heard the rushing of water before they saw it. The River of the Black Pearl. Looming before them. Dark and wide, the outline of the other bank barely visible in the moonlight.

They stopped, and Aurora wondered which way to go. Downstream with the current? Upstream against it? Or back into the forest? But Jah could be anywhere in the tangle of trees.

Mad. Powerful. The white dagger now his.

They both heard the branches snapping as someone moved through the brush. Where was he coming from? Another snap and Aurora decided it was to their left, so she turned right and headed upstream, along the shallow edge of the river.

"Hurry!" she cried. Although they were exposed here, targets in the moonlight, at least they could move more quickly without the trees to block their way.

Speed or cover? Neither would help in the long run.

As they ran onward, their breath coming in gasps, the air burning their throats, she thought the dark shadow looming before her was a trick of her vision. But he was not.

The scream froze in her throat. How had Jah managed to head them off so quickly?

She turned and bumped into Niko. The two stared at each other in horror as the dark shape advanced toward them. They ran back the way they had come, but they were tired and their feet dragged. Aurora glanced over her shoulder. Jah was less than twenty strides away.

He would be able to catch up to them in seconds at this rate.

She kept on, Niko at her heels, but it was no good. Jah was less than ten strides away. Less than the length of a body now. She could see his face clearly, those strange green eyes, the glint of her dagger in his hand. She tried to run faster, but her legs would not go. She could hear Niko's labored breathing. And she could feel without looking that Jah was just behind them.

Maybe she should throw herself on him, try to fight so that at least Niko could get away with the charms. But she wasn't a very good fighter, and she had no weapon without her dagger. Still, it was their only hope.

Just as she was turning toward Jah, Topaz hurtled out of the sky, her staccato cry filling the night.

"Topaz!" Niko gasped as the falcon swooped down on Jah. The Dragon raised his hands to shield his face, but they were no defense against the bird's attack.

"Hurry!" cried Aurora, pulling Niko toward the water. "You can swim, can't you? We can drift downstream with the current. It's our only chance."

Niko nodded dumbly as Jah sliced the air with the white dagger, trying to kill Topaz.

"Give me the charms," Aurora demanded. "If he does find us, he'll expect them to be in your sword." She put them in her pouch as Niko tied the sword to his back with the belt of his tunic.

"Topaz will be all right. Don't worry. Now come on."

With a running leap, Aurora disappeared into the black depths.

Niko stood on the bank, knowing he should follow but unwilling to leave Topaz, whose furious cry echoed in his ears.

"Hurry!" Aurora urged from the water. "She'll find you."

Without another thought Niko dove in, feeling the cold water swallow him. He kicked furiously, propelling himself farther from the shore into the depths of the River of the Black Pearl.

Fly away, Topaz, he thought. A command, a wish, a hope.

CHAPTER 8

Walker pushed open the closet door and looked around. The dressing room was empty. That at least was a relief. He walked to the door and put his eye to the crack. He could see light but no movement. He opened the door a fraction and peered out. No one was in sight.

Walker didn't waste another moment. He jogged down the hallway, noting the high stone ceilings, the plain gray stone of the walls, the small slit windows. It reminded him of the castles his mom had made them visit when they were in England last summer.

She was writing a romance about some English lord who married one of his vassals, and she kept making him stop so she could take notes. Walker pointed out to her that a lord would never marry a vassal during the Middle Ages because of the strict class divisions. But his mom said it didn't matter. It was a love story and love conquered all.

Walker sighed, wishing everything that had happened to him since he picked that charm out of the fountain was just a story. But it wasn't. And he knew it. First things first: to put as much distance between himself and that lord as possible.

"Get out of here, Walker," he whispered, peering down the hall to make sure he was still alone.

Footsteps coming from the left made him decide quickly to go to the right. He ran ahead, but the murmur of voices followed him. What to do? He saw an open door a few feet away and made a dash for it, closing it softly behind him. Close call, he thought with relief.

That was his last thought before someone grabbed him from behind and threw him to the floor.

Walker shook his head and looked up at a tall, dark-haired boy with broad shoulders who was dressed all in white. The boy's brown eyes smoldered as he scowled at Walker. He wore a gold earring, which Walker would have made fun of under ordinary circumstances. But these were not ordinary times.

"Who are you?" The boy spit out the words like a threat, not a question.

Walker had some experience with bullies. He knew he had to answer but also to question, so that the bully would know he was not some loser who would roll over for anybody. "Walker. Who are you?" Walker made the toughest face he could, squinting and drawing his lips into a firm line.

"Everyone calls me Marcus. But you're nothing, just some worm. So you'd best call me sir." He dug his foot hard into Walker's chest. Walker gasped.

"Get off me . . . Marcus."

"What did you call me?"

"Marcus," Walker repeated, glaring up at the bully.

Marcus kicked him, this time in the side. Walker grunted in pain.

"Watch your mouth, worm. I'm warnin' ya. Now, where'd you come from?"

"What's it to you?" Walker retorted.

"What's it to me?" repeated Marcus, with a crazy, crooked smile on his face.

Uh-oh, thought Walker.

"Come on, Olan. Let's teach the new recruit what it means to be a Dragon in training."

Marcus nodded to another boy, who stepped forward, his pale eyes expressionless, like windows opening into an empty room. Together the two boys kicked Walker over and over. Walker groaned. He couldn't help himself.

"That's what it is to me." Marcus spit out the words, grinning horribly. "Ain't that right, Olan?"

The pale-eyed boy laughed, an ugly sound with no humor in it at all.

Angry now, Walker sprang to his feet, ready to fight, but before he could throw a punch, two other boys grabbed him roughly from behind, holding him back. Walker, undeterred, looked Marcus straight in the eye, just like his older brother, Bo, told him to do whenever he met up with a bully, especially one who was a lot bigger. Bo said the more you let a bully know you were afraid, the more he'd hurt you. At least that was his reason for all the fights he used to get into after Dad left.

Walker tried to kick the two boys who were holding him, but they sidestepped him easily, laughing.

"Do ya think that's how they fight where he come from, Almarine?" Marcus sneered to the skinny red-haired boy who held Walker on the right. "He'll never be a Dragon warrior like we're gonna be, eh, Bram?"

"He don't know how to fight," noted Bram, a squat boy with a shaved head, who was holding Walker's left arm. He squeezed Walker's bicep so hard, Walker had to clench his teeth not to cry out.

"Let me go!" said Walker, twisting, trying to free himself. He kicked and elbowed Bram and Almarine, but they only held on tighter, digging their fingernails into his skin. Walker knew it was hopeless—one against four was just not fair odds—but he refused to be bullied. He stared at Almarine's freckled fingers as they clutched his arm, and then he bent and bit the redheaded boy.

Almarine gasped and let go. Walker jerked his other arm free and backed away. Olan, still standing beside Marcus, lunged forward and landed on top of Walker, knocking the wind out of him.

"Get 'im, Olan!" chorused the other boys.

Olan quickly pinned Walker to the floor as Marcus advanced slowly toward him, frowning darkly.

"You gots something I want." He spit out the words.

Walker felt his heart skip a beat. He wouldn't let this bully have the red charm, no matter what.

"So what if I do?" he retorted.

"If I want somethin', then you gotta give it to me," continued Marcus. "'Cause I'm in charge of all the new recruits. And you ain't gonna live to make it to page if you don't listen to me."

"Who says?" countered Walker, more bravely than he felt. Show no fear, he told himself.

"I says," said Olan, twisting Walker's arm until it was bent almost double.

Walker yelped as the pain seared through his shoulder.

"So, gimme your shoes," ordered Marcus. "I ain't never seen shoes like that. And I want 'em."

Walker would have laughed if he hadn't been in so much pain. So this big bully didn't want the charm. He just wanted Walker's high-top sneakers.

"Give 'em to 'im," said Olan through his teeth. He kneed Walker hard in the stomach.

Walker curled up and tried to catch his breath.

"Yeah," echoed the other boys, crowding around, their eyes glinting in the afternoon sunlight, hungrily, like wolves moving in for the kill.

The dormitory door banged open, and two older boys, dressed in red tunics and pants, marched into the room. Walker thought they looked like something out of an old newsreel he'd seen one time of Communist youth in training, with their military bearing, identical clothes, and heavy wooden clubs stuck in their belts. Marcus and the other boys turned and bowed respectfully.

"Did you not hear the bell?" asked the first boy in a monotone. "You are all late for the afternoon training session."

"General Da Gama does not tolerate tardiness from new recruits," added the second boy with a sneer.

Marcus and the others shifted uncomfortably but did not move.

"What are you waiting for, stupid novices?" asked the first boy. "The longer you stay here, the harsher your punishment will be."

Marcus and the other boys tore out of the room, leaving Walker alone with the pages. "Where are your clothes, novice? You cannot go to training dressed like that."

"I'm . . . uh . . . I'm not a novice," began Walker, struggling to his feet. His stomach burned from where Olan had kneed him. He noticed then that there was another boy in the room—a small, skinny boy with hair so fair it looked white, who stood at his elbow. He was holding something white in his arms.

"I don't really belong here," Walker tried to explain as the pages stared at him as if he were speaking a foreign language.

"Yo no soy," Walker began in lame Spanish, thinking it might be worth a try. Spanish was, after all, the fastest-growing language in the world, wasn't it? But it did no good. It only seemed to anger the pages further.

"Get dressed," barked the first one, advancing toward Walker.

The pale-haired boy stepped between them, bowing low before the pages. He pointed to the bundle he was carrying and then to Walker.

"Put on your uniform and report to General Da Gama immediately," ordered the first page.

"I'll stay here with Gibreel and keep an eye on the novice while you continue the patrol," said the second page, his eyes fastened on Walker, his fingers reaching for the club in his belt.

The first page nodded and disappeared through the door.

"But I'm not a novice," Walker began again.

Gibreel nodded as if he understood and unfolded a white tunic and pants, just like the outfits Marcus and the other boys had been wearing. He held them out to Walker, who, after one more look at the page's club, grudgingly put them on. He had no choice, really.

Gibreel smiled and pointed to Walker's high-tops. Had he seen what had just taken place? Walker wondered. He took off his shoes and Gibreel picked them up and walked through the door at the opposite end of the room without saying a word. Walker followed. They stood together in a square stone room, with a row of sinks on one side and a row of metal stalls on the other. Clearly, it was some kind of bathroom.

Gibreel disappeared into the middle stall, where, Walker noted in disgust, there was no toilet—just a hole in the floor. He watched Gibreel push against one of the large stones in the center of the wall. Walker gasped in surprise when the stone moved to reveal darkness beyond. Gibreel shoved Walker's sneakers in the hole in the wall and then carefully pulled the stone back into place.

"What's taking so long?" came the voice of the page, his footsteps echoing on the stones outside the bathroom.

Gibreel put his finger to his lips and smiled at Walker. Hurriedly he bent and opened a low cupboard beside the sinks. He pulled out a pair of brown woven sandals and handed them to Walker.

"Thanks," murmured Walker.

Before he could ask Gibreel anything, the page whisked him down the stairs, through a maze of corridors, and finally outside to a large walled courtyard made of red and brown stone. The walls were high, like prison walls, Walker thought with a sinking feeling in the pit of his stomach. Thick, tall, and smooth.

No good for climbing.

Walker wiped the sweat off his forehead. It was really hot out here. Hot and still, with no trees, just the fiercely burning sun. In the middle of the courtyard stood a very muscular bald man dressed in a red robe. Walker noticed that it was the same man who had come to speak to the lord. He held a long samurai-style sword that glittered sharply in the bright light as he stared at the line of boys before him. Walker picked out Marcus immediately—the bully stood half a head taller than the others. The man turned to Walker, a fierce frown on his face. He looked like an angry bull ready to charge.

"There he is, sir." Marcus's voice rang out in the silent courtyard. "We were only trying to help him, sir. That's why we were late."

The general advanced slowly toward Walker, who stood shifting uncomfortably from foot to foot.

"Get in line!" the general barked. Walker took one look at that sword waving in his direction and ran to the end of the line, just two boys away from his old friends, Olan and Marcus.

"Your name, novice," demanded the bald man.

Walker took a deep breath. Here was his chance

to finally sort out this confusion. All he had to do was explain his situation and the general would realize he did not belong with the recruits. "There seems to have been some kind of mistake."

"Your name!" The general's face reddened and his eyes, which Walker had thought looked angry before, flashed with fury.

"I don't really belong here," began Walker.

The general took one more step closer, his sword still pointing at Walker. "I will decide who belongs here and who doesn't. And if I ever hear you question my authority again, I will cut off one of your fingers to remind you who makes the decisions here. And if you forget once more, I will take another finger and another until you have no fingers left. Then we will have to find other places to cut."

He spoke each word in a calm, even voice, and Walker realized with a shudder that he wasn't kidding. Before he could get over his shock, the general spoke again. "Show him, Olan." The boy raised his hand high in the air, and Walker saw with a sickening lurch of his stomach that he was missing the pinky finger on his right hand.

"Your name, novice!"

"Walker," answered Walker, in a voice that came out sounding more like a croak.

"Wrong," boomed the general.

Walker's eyes widened. How could he be wrong about his own name?

"I am General Da Gama, you worm. Whenever you speak to me, you will address me as 'sir.' Do you understand, worm?"

Walker nodded, feeling about as powerless as a worm that could be cut in half with one careless stroke of the general's sharp sword.

"What did you say?" barked General Da Gama, advancing toward Walker until he stood just a few inches away. Walker could see a gold tooth in his mouth and a long scar that ran in a jagged red line from his neck all the way to his cheek.

"Yes, sir," whispered Walker. What else was he supposed to say, especially if he wanted to hang on to all his fingers?

"I didn't hear you," yelled General Da Gama, his breath hot in Walker's face.

"Yes, sir," Walker said more loudly, fighting the urge to gag as the other boys tittered around him.

"Now do fifty sun salutations."

Walker stared blankly at the general while the other boys laughed. Fifty push-ups, pull-ups, sit-ups, sure . . . maybe. But sun salutations? He'd never heard of those.

"I said, do fifty sun salutations. Now. That's an order."

Walker figured honesty was the best policy. Wasn't that what adults were forever telling you? "I don't know how, sir," he muttered, his heart racing as he watched the point of General Da Gama's sword edge closer to him.

"He doesn't know how," mocked General Da Gama, turning to the other boys, who laughed more loudly now. The general's eyes stopped on Marcus, freezing the boy's smile on his face. "You are amused? Then you can show this worm how to do a sun salutation by doing fifty yourself."

"Yes, sir," answered Marcus, bowing.

Obediently he raised his arms above his head and bent as if he were touching his toes, but he put both palms flat on the ground. He extended first one leg and then the other behind him and did something that looked like a push-up. Then he lay flat, arching his neck up. Quickly he brought his legs back in and stood, and began the whole strange series of movements all over again.

Walker struggled along, aping Marcus's movements as best he could. For such a silly-looking exercise, it was remarkably draining. His arms and legs were shaking with exertion long before he'd done even twenty. He didn't know how he was ever going to make it to fifty.

"Faster, novice!" General Da Gama shouted in his ear.

He tried to move faster, but his arms were shaking so badly, he lost his balance and fell. He scrambled to his feet.

"You may start all over again from one!"

Walker stared at the general in shock as sweat dripped down his face.

"Now, novice!"

Walker didn't know how he managed to do even ten more, let alone fifty. By the end, he was so light-headed he felt as if he might faint. He moved slowly back to his place in line, trying to catch his breath.

"We'll be watching you," Marcus whispered quietly, the threat clear. "Nobody makes us look bad in front of Da Gama."

"Yeah," Olan added, pushing aside the boy between him and Walker. "You gonna be sorry you ever come to the House of the Black Rock. You gonna be sorry you ever was born."

Walker didn't know if he had ever felt as low as he felt at that moment. A stranger in a strange land, with a bunch of bullies and a crazed commando guy all after him. And somewhere out there lurked that lord, an insane maniac running around looking for something Walker had—the one thing that could get him home again. The one thing he couldn't afford to lose.

Instinctively, hardly aware of what he was doing, Walker reached into his pocket, his fingers closing over the smooth, cold square charm. The feel of it somehow gave him strength. Courage.

As long as he had courage, he would be all right. He would get out of this place, wherever it was, and get home. Somehow. Black Rock would be history. A bad dream.

After that he had no more time to think. General Da Gama had them sprint from one end of the courtyard to the other, then jog back, then sprint forward again. Walker, exhausted, could barely keep up. They did push-ups and handstands and played a weird game, a combination of soccer and basketball, in which you had to bounce a ball through a stone hoop six feet high.

Marcus managed to kick Walker more than once. Olan, too. But Walker was too tired to care. They practiced something called the combat stance, where they had to stand with legs firm and head high, concentrating on breathing deeply. It reminded Walker of the weird yoga exercises his mom used to do during her inner peace yoga phase after the divorce.

They did fighting drills, which were like karate matches, involving lots of side kicks and hand motions. And sword drills with sticks. Hours passed before the sun began to set, casting the courtyard in shadow. All Walker wanted was to sit down for a minute and drink something cold. He could practically taste the soda, sweet and refreshing, hear the ice cubes clinking in the glass.

"Worm!" General Da Gama's voice brought him up with a start. "How many times must I call your name before you hear me?"

An infinite number, thought Walker, since *worm* is not my name.

"Daydreaming, are you?"

Walker didn't answer, just hurried to the end of the line the boys had formed before the general, breathing deeply so as not to lose his temper. He watched as General Da Gama withdrew a key from the pouch at his waist and unlocked the gate.

"Now run until I tell you to stop," ordered the general.

Walker wondered how he was supposed to run when he could barely walk. He followed the other boys slowly through the stone gate. What he saw then made him forget his exhaustion, forget all his aches and pains from the fight with Marcus, forget even the brutality of General Da Gama. For all around him stretched desert, miles and miles of desolate, windswept sand, with nothing else in sight.

How, Walker wondered desperately, will I ever get out of here?

CHAPTER 9

Niko rubbed his neck, stiff from sleeping with his head propped against the wooden seat of the boat. Aurora lay beside him, her knees tucked under her for warmth, her long hair spread over her like a blanket. He blinked as the unfamiliar landscape rolled by.

It was a stroke of luck that they had found this sailboat, battered though it was, for they never would have made it otherwise. Not two of them hanging on to one flimsy branch. Niko shook his head, remembering. The cracking of the wood, Aurora screaming, both of them being pulled by the current, swirling through the dark water, hurtling toward the shore, into something hard.

This old sailboat. Once quite plush, Niko thought, for the seats had the remains of velvet covers. And the wood was good balsa, smooth and polished.

Some would say luck had brought them to the boat. Others might call it chance. Or destiny if they believed in predetermination, like the master, who said everything happened for a reason.

Niko sighed, staring up at the scattering of stars and the moon, a sliver of silver in the sky. His eyes roamed the black expanse, searching for a familiar dark winged shape. It was a reflex, like breathing. Losing Topaz was the very opposite of luck. So was losing the master. And Ruah. There could be no good reason for things like that to happen.

Everyone he loved in the world was gone.

He closed his eyes, feeling the rocking of the boat. A memory suddenly came to him of the time long ago when he and the master had sailed to the Island of the Five Mountains. He didn't know why he thought of it now. But he was powerless to stop remembering, as images flooded his mind, taking him back.

He was a little boy of six or seven, his hair long. Lord Amber wrapped a cloth around his eyes.

"Master, why do you blindfold me?"

"So that you will be able to navigate to the Island of the Five Mountains in your mind."

He and the master paddled for days, through water that was calm and water that was rough, through the heat of the day and the chill of the night. At first he desperately wanted to take off the blindfold, but in time he became so used to it, he barely noticed the blindness, for he could "see" with his other senses. He could hear and smell the island before they got there, feel its presence in the depth of his being, the same way he could tell when Topaz was near, with the instinctive consciousness that comes from the heart. Niko knew with absolute certainty that he could get to the island again, though he would never be able to identify it on any map.

When they reached the island, he and Lord Amber began a long climb up a mountain. Niko's legs ached as he struggled to keep pace, yet his footing was sure despite the blindfold his master forbade him to remove. When they neared the top, he felt the master stiffen beside him. Then the stones began to hit them. They weren't big stones, but they hurt. Lord Amber continued on unaffected, almost as if he did not feel the stones striking him, but Niko began to cry.

"Master, why do they throw stones at us? Do they not want us to come?"

"Quite the opposite. They want to make sure that we

desire to come beyond our mere human form—that our hearts desire this. The stones ward off those who are not pure in spirit."

Niko gritted his teeth to stop the pain, determined to reach the top.

He must have fallen asleep, because when he opened his eyes, the boat was still, wedged between two leafless trees growing crookedly out of the water. Niko didn't know where they were, and it was difficult to make anything out, for the mist hung low, a swirling, drifting white fog. Occasionally it lifted like a curtain, revealing a tall, dense forest that seemed to grow into the river itself.

He scrambled to the side of the boat and tried to push it free. But it was stuck fast in a tangle of roots. He needed something to push off with. A branch would do the trick. There had to be a fallen one somewhere nearby. He looked down at Aurora, still sleeping. He thought about waking her but decided against it. He would be right back. And if she were up, she would insist on braving the forest with him. To protect him. He certainly didn't need her to do that. He could take care of it by himself. After all, he was the Chooser and a warrior—almost. And warriors didn't have protectors, especially not girls.

Quietly he reached for the silver sword.

He eased himself off the boat, taking care not to

wake Aurora with sudden motion. He moved toward the impenetrable woods before him. You can do it, he told himself. You don't need a protector. You don't need anybody. It's just a bunch of trees. Nothing to be afraid of.

Gripping the sword more tightly, he stepped into the darkness. He could barely see, so he bent lower to the ground, feeling with his fingers. He moved forward, still searching. A sound somewhere behind him made him jump. It's just an animal, he told himself, lost in the dark or looking for food. But he heard the sound again, deliberate in the darkness.

Don't be afraid, he told himself. He took a few more steps.

Thc sound came again, closer this time. "Who's there?" he whispered, holding his sword before him.

There was no answer.

He took another step toward a large tree in front of him. At its base he saw what looked like a bunch of sticks. There had to be one there that he could use. He was hurrying toward it when suddenly his foot caught in some kind of noose and he was jerked up in the air, swinging wildly in the darkness.

He pushed and pulled, trying to free himself, but the more he struggled, the tighter the noose became. The rope dug into his skin, and he could feel a warm trickle of what had to be blood around his ankle.

Don't panic, he told himself. You still have the sword. You can cut yourself loose. As he was about to swing himself upward to reach the rope, three of the dirtiest men he had ever seen entered the clearing. They looked more like beasts in their greasy animal-skin breeches and their long matted hair. Sheathed in their belts he saw long sharp knives. One of the men carried an ax with rusty streaks—the color of dried blood.

"Lookee here," said the biggest of the men, who had a ragged yellow beard that hung down to his chest. "Lookee what we got."

The other two, one with a red beard, the other dark-haired, nodded, and their mouths turned up at the corners. What few teeth they had looked brown and rotten. The red beard grabbed Niko's sword and began to stroke it with dirt-stained fingers.

"Gimme that," ordered the big blond man.

The red beard shrugged and tossed the sword to the bigger man, who caught it in hands the size of melons. Hands that looked as if they could crush Niko with one squeeze. "What should we do with 'im?" red beard asked, advancing toward the upside-down Niko. "I's hungry."

The other two murmured, staring at Niko with pale, empty eyes. Niko gulped. Oh, no, he thought.

To be killed by his own sword and then eaten by these cannibals . . .

Red beard and the dark-haired man laughed.

"He looks tasty, right, Red?" yellow hair said.

Niko tried to swallow, but he had a lump in his throat so big he was afraid he would choke. He had read about bands of wild cannibals. He'd never dreamed he would meet any. If only he hadn't left the boat. But it was too late for that now.

The leader stepped closer to Niko, and Niko could smell his nasty, sour breath. Niko gagged as yellow hair thrust the silver sword, his sword, the sword of Janus, toward his throat, its sharp blade glinting in the moonlight.

Aurora had been having the strangest dream. Even awake, its memory lingered in full detail. She was running along a narrow, dusty road in a hot, dry place. In front of her was a frieze carved in the red sandstone of a mountain, of a procession of animals—camels maybe, it was hard to tell. Someone was chasing her and she had to find the Empress, who was somewhere behind the frieze. She could hear her screaming and a baby crying. The Empress's baby, Aurora thought. Aurora had to reach them before she was caught, but she could hear footsteps behind her. She ran faster. Suddenly she saw the Empress, holding a slashed and bloodied jeweled slipper. A strange blue-green light glowed around her. In her other arm she held her baby. Above her the full moon rose in the darkening sky.

But it wasn't a white moon. It was red.

Red moon rising, thought Aurora. That meant something, but she didn't know what.

She turned to ask Niko, but he was not there. She saw with surprise that his sword was gone too. And the boat was still, moored between two twisted trees. She shivered. She didn't like the misty water and the tall dark trees. It was the kind of place where gasts roamed, spirits of the dead who sucked life out of the living, who slid into your body and took over your mind without ever even being seen.

"Niko!" she called in a soft voice. "Where are you?"

There was no answer. Aurora scrambled to her feet. Where had he gone, and why would he have left her? She tried to suppress a growing feeling of annoyance—and panic. She didn't think it was a good idea for him to wander off. He didn't know these woods at all, and he wasn't a tracker. He could be lost in a heartbeat. He's probably just a few feet away in the forest and didn't hear me, she told herself. Cautiously she stepped out of the boat, wading through the swampy water and up onto the bank. The forest rose before her, dark and forbidding.

"Niko!" she called again, this time more loudly. "This isn't funny."

Again there was no answer. She'd heard stories of forests like this one, great lonely places where people wandered in circles for days till they disappeared, swallowed up by the mist and the trees, or maybe by the gasts. This was nothing like the friendly forest near the Gypsy camp that she loved so well. Aurora walked farther but saw no sign of life, no sign of Niko.

"Niko!" She tried one last time.

But the wind had picked up, carrying her voice with it, shrieking through the trees. She shivered, and hugged herself for warmth. Where had this wind come from? It was enough to blow their sailboat well on its way. Oh, no, Aurora gasped. The charms! She'd left them in the boat, along with the Empress's chart of the Doors of the Hunab Ku. She turned and ran from the haunted moonlit forest back toward the boat, hoping Niko had returned. But he hadn't.

And the boat was drifting away from the shore, borne along by the wind-whipped current and rising tide.

She splashed through the cold water toward the dark, bobbing shape that was slipping farther away from her. She pushed forward against the current, grasping the trees to support herself, and managed to grab hold of the boat. She threw herself over the edge and landed in the bottom as the current pulled the boat into the middle of the river, away from the forest—and Niko.

Aurora stared at the landscape rapidly rolling by and her eyes filled with tears. She held the purple pouch full of charms in her hands and rocked back and forth, shivering in her wet dress. Some Protector she was. She had lost the Chooser, whom it was her job to protect. And one of the charms. And she'd almost lost the remaining eight.

Maybe Niko was right—a girl couldn't be the Protector. The real Protector would never have made the mess of things that she had. She hung her head, crying earnestly now, her body shaking with sobs.

After a few minutes, she looked up and the breath caught in her throat. A strange glowing form was rising out of the swirling mist. Long golden hair entwined with green leaves. Pale skin covered by a dress made of a shimmering green-blue fabric. But it was the eyes that captured Aurora. Shining eyes so blue they could not possibly be human.

They were the eyes of a gast, out to devour her soul.

"There is no reason for you to be afraid," soothed a tinkling voice that sounded like water trickling over rocks. Of nature, yet not natural. It was as if the river itself had found a voice in this shimmering green creature.

Aurora edged to the opposite end of the boat, as far from the ghostly vision as she could get. She tried to stop staring into those glittering eyes, but they held her as light holds a moth.

"It's all right, Aurora. Please, do not fear me," insisted the gentle, dancing voice.

Aurora's breath came in frightened gasps. This spirit knew her name. It was probably taking over her soul at this very moment. "Leave me alone, gast!" She choked out the words.

The green-blue creature began to laugh then, a bubbling brook of joy, gentle and musical and not menacing at all. Aurora frowned. This was probably some trick the gasts used to lull you into thinking they weren't dangerous.

"I am not a gast, child. I am Calliope, Sister of the Kuxan-Sunn. You must listen to me, for my sisters will soon notice I am gone."

"Why should I listen to you?" Aurora retorted, her back pressed against the edge of the boat, ready to jump off and swim to safety if need be. "I've never heard of the Sisters of the Kuxan-Sunn."

"No, you have not. For we are not of your world. We live between the worlds, guardians of the pathways, part spirit and part flesh, able to enter any world at will but forbidden to live in any one place. Like my sisters, I can see the future and the past. I am here because I have known of the coming of the Chooser and the Protector for a long, long time."

"You have?" The words rolled off Aurora's tongue before she could stop them.

"And of the Bearer of the charm of fire and blood."

Aurora thought back to the charm she had dropped in the water.

"Do you mean the red charm?"

Calliope nodded.

"Has someone come?"

Calliope studied Aurora intently before she finally spoke. "Yes, Protector, he has come."

"But how can that be?" Aurora gasped in surprise. "I lost that charm. I dropped it in the water and it disappeared. Just like I lost Niko. I can't really be the Protector. I think maybe it's all a big mistake. Just be—"

"Raise your right hand," Calliope interrupted in a firm voice that Aurora couldn't help obeying.

The Dragon's Eye mark was clearly visible on Aurora's palm, the dark triangle with the circle inside it.

"Sign of the Dragon's Eye, great will be her sight," recited Calliope. "You bear the sign. Is it not also true that you have the sight?"

"I cannot see into the future and the past, as you say you can."

"That is different, for I am not human as you are. My sight is limited. Yours is unbound. For it comes to you in your dreams, doorways to all the worlds. Through dreams you can see into the eternal present, the now that is past and future combined, two streams that flow into one river. You can affect by your choices and your actions the outcome of many things. That I cannot do."

"This eternal present . . . I don't understand."

"Your dreams are for you to understand," Calliope insisted. "I cannot teach you that which I do not know. You *are* the Protector, Aurora, of all that is good and all that is light. Look to your dreams and follow the signs."

"What signs? What do you mean?"

Calliope's image began to shimmer in the moonlight and then to fade.

"You will know."

"How will I know?"

"Remember your dreams. And beware others like me."

The blood sang in Aurora's ears. She suddenly remembered her dream of the twisting mountain road, the oppressive heat, the strange frieze. The Empress with the bloody slipper, and the red moon rising.

"The Empress!" gasped Aurora.

But Calliope had vanished into the moonlit mist, leaving Aurora alone with the bag of charms and the Empress's indecipherable chart of the Doors of the Hunab Ku, drifting along the dark water, borne by the current into the night.

CHAPTER 10

Sweat dripped down Walker's forehead and into his eyes. All around him the heat shimmered in the afternoon air. He stopped walking and shifted the heavy wooden water buckets from one shoulder to the other. Raising one hand to his eyes, he scanned the desolate desert landscape.

The House of the Black Rock was nowhere in sight.

That meant he had at least a mile to go. Probably more. He sighed. It was bad enough being stuck in this strange other world, but being General Da

Gama's favorite target was just too much. This was his second trip to the spring, which was at least five miles away. The other novices had already finished, but General Da Gama had decided that Walker had spilled too much water. So he had sent him back, even though he'd seen with his own two eyes that Olan had spilled a whole bucket of water, and Bram, too. Da Gama's special persecution of Walker continued every day. Yesterday he'd had to do an extra hour of kick drills because General Da Gama said he wasn't extending his legs high enough or hitting the bag hard enough. Walker had thought his legs were going to break. Today he'd barely been able to get out of bed because they ached so badly.

Walker began walking once more, gritting his teeth in determination. He'd been at Black Rock for five days now, but this was his last, as far as he was concerned. Tonight was the night. He was breaking out.

He'd heard some of the boys talking about a city. He didn't know how far away it was, but he was going to get there. Somehow. He figured it would be a better place to hide from that crazy lord and that weird sister and whoever else might be after his charm. And he felt certain he could find someone in a city to help him get home.

All he had to do was escape. He didn't allow

himself to think about what might happen if he got caught.

"Move, novice!" ordered a page on a speckled black-and-white pony, who galloped to Walker's side.

Walker rolled his eyes, muttering under his breath, but he began to walk more quickly. There was no point in getting a page mad, because he'd just tell General Da Gama, and that would only make Walker's situation worse. The pages were a level above the novices. They were mostly fifteen and sixteen, and they were allowed to make the novices' lives miserable. Da Gama even encouraged it. They were all training for a ceremony called the Five Fires. Walker heard Almarine talking about it to Marcus. You had to walk over flaming coals without burning your feet, and if you did it, they made you a Dragon.

It sounded pretty sick to Walker. And just up General Da Gama's alley. But all the boys were psyched. They couldn't wait to be pages and then Dragons. Apparently the Dragons were the fiercest warriors around, with their swords and metal tubes called flamethrowers. No one in this world seemed to have ever seen a gun or heard of nuclear warheads. They thought sword fighting was the most dangerous kind of combat.

Walker also gathered that their training was a big-deal secret, kind of like FBI Special Forces, which was why they had set up shop in the desert. He sighed and looked up. In the distance the walls of Black Rock rose before him, dark and forbidding, their long shadows reaching toward him across the sand. He watched as the sun slowly began to sink behind those black walls. Oh, no, he thought. If he wasn't back before the sun had completely set, General Da Gama's punishment would be severe.

Carefully, balancing the water buckets between his shoulders, he began to run. Closer and closer, the walls loomed over him now. Just a few more steps. He was almost there and he hadn't spilled a drop. Well, maybe a drop, but no more than that.

When he was almost at the gate, it swung open. And there stood Marcus, flanked by Bram, Olan, Almarine, and a whole bunch of the other novices.

Great, thought Walker. This was definitely not a welcoming committee.

"You're late, water boy," Marcus taunted.

Walker gritted his teeth, determined not to fight.

"Yeah, water boy," echoed Olan as he and Marcus stepped closer.

"Let's see those buckets," ordered Marcus.

Walker stepped forward, ignoring them, trying to work his way toward the entrance as precious seconds ticked by. An image of Olan's missing pinky stole into Walker's mind and he gulped. He had to get the water to Da Gama. This was no game.

"I said show me the buckets, worm."

And before Walker could move away, Olan and Marcus each bumped into one of the buckets. Water slopped over the sides and spilled onto the sand.

"Oh, no," crooned Marcus. "How clumsy of me." He laughed and the other boys laughed with him.

"Wait till Da Gama finds out," crowed Olan.

"You're gonna get it," added Bram.

"And you thought you was so tough," crooned Marcus, lounging against the wall.

Suddenly Walker didn't care that Marcus was twice his size. He didn't care about Da Gama's punishment or keeping out of trouble. He didn't care about escaping. All he could think about was not letting this bully make a fool of him.

"You son of a . . . ," Walker yelled as he dropped the buckets and leaped at Marcus, swinging his fists wildly. Marcus, laughing still, was caught off guard and turned too late to step out of Walker's way. Walker's fist connected, hitting Marcus squarely in the jaw.

A shocked murmur ran through the crowd of

boys. No one picked a fight with Marcus, especially not a second time.

Marcus wiped a spot of blood from his mouth and advanced toward Walker, dangerously deliberate. He grabbed Walker by the collar of his tunic and twisted the material tight in his choking fist.

"Get 'im, Marcus!" shouted Olan. "He'll never live to be a Dragon."

"Yeah," chorused the other boys, crowding closer.

Marcus shook Walker by the collar. Walker's eyes bugged out and he gasped for air.

"Get 'im good!" shouted a voice as the other boys took up the chant.

"Make it hurt!" jeered another.

Walker's arms flailed helplessly at his sides as he struggled to breathe. He barely noticed a small figure crawling behind Marcus. Gibreel! He looked up at Walker, catching his eye. Walker wondered what he was doing, crawling like that, when it hit him.

Walker waited for Marcus to cock his fist back and then lunged forward and pushed with all his might. Marcus, taken by surprise, stepped back to keep his balance and tripped over Gibreel, who was crouching behind him. With a thud, Marcus fell heavily to the stones. Walker's momentum continued to send him forward, and he tripped over Gibreel too, crashing down on top of Marcus.

At that moment footsteps sounded on the flagstones and General Da Gama appeared, bald head shining in the torchlight, his expression fierce. Before Walker could move, General Da Gama yanked him up and threw him hard against the stone wall.

"What is going on here?" he demanded in a low, angry voice.

"It was two against one, sir," said Olan, pointing to Walker and Gibreel.

"Gibreel, you know you are forbidden to associate with the novices. You are here only to serve them. And if you can't do that, then . . ." He let his voice trail off, and in that pause, terrible things that might happen to Gibreel popped into Walker's mind. How could he let the only person who had been kind to him get in trouble because of him? But then again, if he said something, he'd only get in more trouble. And he was in more than enough trouble already. He debated with himself for a moment.

"He didn't do anything," Walker said. "It was my fault . . . sir," he added.

The general stared at Walker with his flat, cold shark eyes as if he hadn't spoken. "Where is the water I sent you for?"

Walker pointed to the buckets, one of which was

overturned, the other less than a quarter full. He gulped, "There, sir."

"You have failed again," began General Da Gama, his mouth twisted in a cruel leer, "and this time you will be properly disciplined."

The thundering of hooves on the sand and the echoing cries of the pages galloping toward Black Rock interrupted Da Gama. Through the bars of the gate, Walker could see a group of red-clad figures riding hard and fast on their little ponies, herding something forward.

"Open the gates!" cried a guard.

General Da Gama waved his arms, gesturing at Marcus and Olan, who ran over and threw the gates wide. Walker watched, figuring they had probably caught some kind of desert animal, grateful that he was no longer the focus of the general's anger. Maybe all the commotion would make Da Gama forget about Walker and whatever punishment he was cooking up in that cue-ball head of his. Walker dropped back as the boys around him surged forward, all eager to see what the pages had caught in the barren desert.

The boys nearest him sprang back, gasping.

"What is it?" someone asked.

"The Black Asha," murmured someone else.

"Like in the stories," said a voice.

"What stories?"

"Don't you remember the story of the Black Ashas? The five black mares who belonged to the Grand High Lord of Time. They were stolen and locked up by the Lords of the Dark, who gave them no food or water for seven days. And when the Grand High Lord of Time, who was busy battling the Lords of the Dark, was finally able to come to their rescue, he tried to feed them, but they wouldn't pause to drink or eat. They followed him into battle and fought alongside the other Lords of Time. Because of them the Lords of Time won the war and the Lords of the Dark couldn't stop time."

"That's just a myth. It ain't real."

"'Tis real, all right," mumbled another. "Look for yourselves. That is no ordinary animal. 'Tis one of the Black Ashas for sure."

Walker pressed forward to see. In the midst of the desert ponies reared a wild black horse, mouth frothing, trying desperately to escape the narrowing circle of pages. It was the biggest horse Walker had ever seen, snorting wildly, its back wet with sweat.

General Da Gama motioned for one of the pages to come to him at the same moment that Walker was pushed forward by the crowd. He wound up just behind the general, stuck in a corner, unable to move away. And quite able to hear what the general was whispering to the page.

"Tell him the Black Asha has come. She is here. The prophecy is fulfilled."

What prophecy? Walker wondered. He was pretty sure, though, that "him" could only be the mysterious lord. Walker hadn't seen the man since that time in the closet. But even though he hadn't laid eyes on him since then, Walker had the feeling that he was around every corner, peering out a window, somehow knowing all that occurred.

The page ran across the courtyard and disappeared into one of the buildings. The shouting grew louder, and Walker saw that the black horse was almost at the gates now, pushed forward by the charging herd of ponies. Suddenly she changed direction, veering sharply to the left. She charged into the unsuspecting ponies, who snorted in fright and threw their pages to the ground. The horse galloped away from the gates of Black Rock and had almost broken free when a fresh wave of pages appeared from the rear of the charge and surrounded her once more, hemming her in so tightly on all sides that she could not break through again.

Walker and the other boys jumped back as the black horse charged into the courtyard, her neighing cries echoing off the stones.

"Catch it!" ordered General Da Gama, throwing a coil of rope toward the boys. Bram reached up and caught it.

"Give it here!" barked Marcus, grabbing the rope from his hands. He stepped closer to the black beast, who pawed the ground with such force that sparks flew from the stones. Then he swung the rope in a circle above his head, but before he could let it fly, the Black Asha reared and knocked the novices closest to her to the ground. She charged straight for Marcus, who had no time to fall back before he too was knocked down.

After that the Black Asha galloped around the courtyard in a frenzy. Pages, novices, and guards fell back as she charged their way. Walker stood frozen in his corner. Her raw power and energy, her wildness, were so strange within the military confines of Black Rock.

"Rope her!" demanded General Da Gama, tossing the novices another rope.

Almarine caught it this time. He turned helplessly to face the charging animal.

"Gimme that rope!" yelled Marcus, blood running down the side of his face.

Walker shook his head. Marcus was crazy, he thought. That horse was going to kill him.

Everyone watched Marcus as he stepped forward

again, his dark eyes as wild as the eyes of the frightened horse. Twirling the rope in a wide arc, Marcus threw it for the second time. But the Black Asha managed to sidestep it by a hairsbreadth, darting away once more.

"That's the craziest horse I ever seen," breathed Olan.

Walker had to agree. He watched as the pages circled the horse once more, trying to lasso her in the cramped courtyard. But the Black Asha would not let herself be caught. She ran like the wind, darting now left, now right, never tiring.

She stopped suddenly and a hush fell over the crowd. Then she began to run hard toward Walker's corner, her huge eyes rolling wildly in their sockets. This time Marcus and the others screamed and ran out of the way. But Walker, with his back to the wall, had nowhere to go.

The Black Asha was heading right for him.

His mouth opened in a wide O of horror, the scream frozen in his throat as the massive beast charged closer and closer. He closed his eyes, waiting for the sickening, lurching thud of the impact, but it never came. At the last moment, just before she would have crushed him to death, the Black Asha reared high on her hind legs, her whinnying cry echoing off the flagstones. Walker felt the wind whistling past his ears as her sharp hooves just missed grazing his cheek.

He was going to die. Crushed to death by a wild horse. Of all the ways to go, he'd never imagined an end like this.

But the Asha didn't crush him. Instead she nuzzled him with her great black nose. He heard the gasping voices all around him, the murmurs of shock. At the same moment, he felt a sudden warmth on the right side of his body, a flash of heat that dissolved the coldness of his fear. He reached into his pocket, and his fingers grasped the charm, the cold metal now warm to the touch. In a flash he realized that the charm and the horse belonged together. The Black Asha had come to free him.

Walker took a deep breath, and stared into the wild black eyes. He'd only taken a few pony rides when he was little, but his mom was a good rider. He remembered her telling him a trick she'd pulled once on a horse that had gone crazy at a show when she was a kid. It was worth a try. Keeping his eyes locked with the Asha's, he leaned up and blew into her nostrils.

"What's he doin'?" Walker heard Bram murmur.

"He's gonna get hisself killed," said Olan.

"He's crazy," added Marcus. "That horse'll crush 'im to death."

But she didn't. Instead, she nuzzled Walker once more. Shocked silence descended on the crowd until General Da Gama thundered, "Rope the Black Asha, boy!"

Someone threw Walker a rope, but he never caught it. Instead, he buried his hands in her long, black mane and pulled himself onto her back. He leaned forward and crouched against her neck, his hands gripping her mane. He felt her heart beating wildly in time with his own. "Come on, girl!" he whispered.

The horse understood and galloped through the barrier of startled pages, away from General Da Gama's angry face and the astonished looks of the other novices. Away from the shadow eyes at the window.

With one swift movement, General Da Gama pulled out his sword and cut the ropes of the massive gate. Walker's eyes widened in horror as the horse thundered toward the rapidly closing gates; she could not get through in time.

"No!" yelled Walker, his voice mingling with the Asha's scream of fury. The Black Asha reared, her hooves beating helplessly against the heavy wood of the gates. After that all Walker knew was blackness.

CHAPTER 11

"Get up, boy!"

Walker awoke startled, staring at the dark shapes bobbing in and out of the murky orange torchlight. He stumbled to his feet but then fell as someone pushed him back down onto cold, wet stones.

"Move!" someone else ordered, prodding Walker with something hard and sharp.

Walker struggled to stand and then to walk. He had no idea how much time had passed since he had fallen off the black horse. Maybe it was an hour, maybe it was a day. He licked his lips and the salty taste of blood came off on his tongue. He put up a hand and felt a lump on his head, which throbbed under his touch, as the Dragons herded him down the long stone hallway and up a steep flight of steps.

"Where are you taking me?" he asked.

"Quiet!" shouted one of the guards. He shoved Walker through a door, where the boy fell to his knees. Torches glared all around, blinding him. He raised his hands to shield his eyes. Goose bumps rose on his arms, either from the cold night wind or from the fear that was growing like a knot in his stomach, he couldn't tell which.

"Ah, the great warrior who rode the Black Asha." General Da Gama's voice was menacing. "How good of you to join us for our evening training session."

Walker blinked again, and his eyes finally adjusted to the light. General Da Gama stood over him. At his signal two pages came forward and helped remove his long robe, revealing his bare chest. Walker noticed the way his muscles rippled. Scanning the circle of lights in panic, Walker noted for the first time that he was in the center of a ring of novices and pages, all crowded around and waiting expectantly. Expecting what? Walker wondered.

"One with such riding skills must surely have other secrets."

General Da Gama's voice washed over him like a blast of icy water. He watched in alarm as the general circled him like a shark, his eyes never leaving Walker's face.

"Show us your secret fighting skills."

Walker swallowed once, but he didn't say anything. Maybe silence would prompt General Da Gama to leave him alone. Maybe not.

"Well, boy? What is your specialty? The ax?"

What would anybody do with an ax besides chop wood? Walker wondered. On second thought, he didn't want to know. But he had a sinking feeling that he was about to find out. He watched as the general reached behind him and picked up a large wood-handled ax from an assortment of weapons stuck in the sand. He swung the weapon in a low arc. Walker snapped his eyes shut, sure his head was about to be cut off. The ax came so close, he could smell the iron it was made of.

When he finally dared to open his eyes, General Da Gama was still swinging the ax, but over his head now in wide circles. Walker could hear the blade cutting the air. The general released the ax and Walker watched in horror as it flew right over his body, heading for the crowd of boys. He almost called out, sure that someone would die. But no one else screamed. And a few seconds later, a heavy thud signaled that the ax had hit something hard.

"Get up!"

Walker stumbled to his feet. A page came forward, carrying a long wooden pole decorated with an inlaid mother-of-pearl design. General Da Gama twirled the pole effortlessly from one hand to the other, his eyes still on Walker.

"Perhaps the bo is your weapon. Take it!" ordered Da Gama, suddenly hurling the pole. Walker lunged forward, just managing to catch it. "We will learn your secrets, worm."

The general closed his eyes, planted his feet firmly in the sand, and began to move his hands in a series of graceful motions.

"Attack!"

Walker hesitated. What kind of trap was this? He caught Marcus's eye and looked quickly away, but not before he had seen the gloating expression on his enemy's dark face.

"Attack!"

This time Walker lunged forward, the pole thrust before him like a spear, but before he put his foot down, the general swept his leg back with a lightning kick. Walker crashed to the ground, facefirst. He could hear the boys laughing, especially Marcus's husky jeer, which was louder and more mocking than the others. His ears burned as the blood pumped furiously through his body.

"No secret attack weapons?" taunted the general, eyes still closed, hands barely moving as if in slow motion. "No special moves you would like to teach us?"

Walker grabbed the pole again, determined to hit General Da Gama this time. But before he could swing, the general jumped in the air and gracefully, almost casually, kicked him in the chest. The impact sent Walker flying into the crowd of boys, who pushed him back to the center of the circle. This time the general attacked without pause and kicked him in the stomach. Walker fell and clutched his gut, his breath coming in short, fast gasps.

"Get up!"

Walker tried to raise his head, but he couldn't.

"I said, get up, worm!"

But Walker, still gasping for breath, just lay there, his face buried in the sand. The general grabbed him roughly by the hair, jerking his head up.

"You have no secrets, boy. And no special skills. Remember this the next time you think of running away. If you are foolish enough to even try, you'll be dead. You can count on that."

The tower bell began to ring, its tones echoing in the silent courtyard. General Da Gama signaled for his robe, which two pages draped over his shoulders.

"Fall in!" shouted a Dragon. "To the dining hall!"

"Except for you," General Da Gama said, tapping Walker on the head with the sole of his boot. "You will help feed the prisoners and see what horrors await you if you dare try anything else. Perhaps we'll discover you're more useful to us as a servant than a warrior."

Walker lay on the ground, blinking dazedly, watching the other boys line up behind General Da Gama. As soon as the general's back was turned, Marcus bent over him.

"You finally got what you deserved," he whispered in Walker's ear. Then he stood and spit on Walker. "Worm!" The word rang in Walker's ears.

Walker only managed to wave his fist weakly as Marcus walked away. One day he would get even with General Da Gama and the Dragons and all the sniveling novices who had reduced him to this beat-up pulp. He tried to pull himself up but fell again. Gibreel appeared at his side to help him to his feet, silent as usual. One look at the quiet sympathy in those pale brown eyes and thoughts of vengeance flew from Walker's mind, reminding him of what really mattered—finding a way home.

CHAPTER 12

It was early morning when Aurora reached the outskirts of the City of Sand and Stone. She could see the buildings rising up, dark silhouettes in the yellow haze of the dawn. And she could hear the far-off sound of voices floating toward her on the wind, as fishing boats sailed out from the harbor and cargo vessels docked to unload their goods.

It had taken more than a day for the river to bring her here. An image of the bloody slipper flashed through her mind, and she hoped she wasn't too late. Calliope hadn't explained about the timing of her dreams. Had she dreamed the past or was it the future? Either way, she'd have to hurry. She'd failed once as the Protector. She couldn't fail again.

She'd never been to the city before, but she knew the palace was on the water. Titi had told her once of the beautiful fireworks the Emperor would set off, before the War of the Flowers. Before he got sick and the dark times came.

As she drew closer, boats began to pass her, and she noticed with a growing sense of alarm that as they did the fishermen or sailors on deck would look over at her and bow, taking off their hats, and bending their heads. The extravagant show of respect troubled her. She was only a girl in a small boat with no interesting goods to sell. Why the courtly gestures?

She took a deep breath. She was just nervous, that was all. This bowing was probably some city custom or a gesture of friendship between sailors. Or so she thought until one fisherman raised his eyes to the sail of her boat and immediately dropped to his knees. She stared up at the sail, and then it struck her. She clapped her hand to her mouth. The sail was purple, branding this an imperial craft! And she and Niko had never noticed.

All these people thought she was connected to the royal family.

Aurora wiped her sweaty palms on her dress. She

breathed deeply again, air in one nostril and out the other. She had to stay calm or she would lose her awareness, and Titi always told her that a person without awareness was like a horse and cart without a driver, going nowhere. First things first. She had to ditch the boat before someone realized she was not a courtier and she was arrested for stealing.

Her thoughts were interrupted as the tide of the ocean collided with the current of the river and the boat suddenly spun around and headed toward the open sea. Quickly she turned the sail to catch the wind, and the boat changed course, back toward the bustling harbor. She crossed her fingers, hoping that no one would question her.

As she sailed farther into the harbor, she could feel more and more eyes on her. She was afraid to try to dock in the midst of all the cargo and fishing boats because she'd never docked a boat before and she didn't know how well she could control it. Everyone would know for sure the imperial craft wasn't hers.

She was scanning the bustling harbor with mounting panic when she noticed a small wooden dock separate from the main pier. It was falling apart, the planks splintered from wind and weather, and there was no activity. The perfect place to ditch a boat.

Aurora tugged the sail one way and then the other, trying to guide the boat. She was so busy that she didn't notice the boys who were sitting on the pilings until the boat bumped into the dock and she almost hit one of them. She looked up in surprise, meeting the cool, appraising glance of a boy not much older than she. Behind him two more boys stared at her. As they moved closer she saw a knife in one boy's belt.

"Morning," said the first boy, running a hand through his slicked-back fair hair.

Aurora tried to appear calm. She didn't like the way this boy was staring at her. She noticed a moon-shaped red scar on the boy's right cheek. It made her uneasy. Something about those eyes and his moon-shaped scar pricked her memory.

As she glanced around the harbor, searching for somewhere else to dock, the sun bounced off the water and blinded her for a moment, ripples of light glancing off the dark surface. The saltwater smell mingled with the odor of fish, and a wave of memory engulfed her, so strong she staggered backward, almost losing her grip on the sail.

She *had* been here in the City of Sand and Stone. Once, a long time ago. She had been so small that she'd been holding Titi's hand. There was something in the water. Someone was making her look at it—

the boy with the scar. Something floating under the bridge. She remembered crying and the sun shining off the water the same way it was now. Shining into her eyes so that she had to close them tight. Holding Titi's hand so hard that it hurt. Her mother was gone, she had known then.

There was nowhere else to dock, so Aurora jumped out, landing lightly, ready to run. But before she could move, the boy with the scar clasped her roughly by the shoulder.

"Serge is the name," he said, smiling. "This here is Brasi." He pointed to a tall boy wearing a black cap and black pants. "That's Noe." He nodded at the third boy, who stared at Aurora impassively, playing with something in his hands.

It was the knife, Aurora realized.

"We keep our eyes on anything that comes in or out of the harbor," said Serge, extending his hand. "Know what I mean?"

Aurora stared at him, backing slowly away, feeling like a bird trapped by a cat.

"Nice little boat," he said, studying it. "Purple sail and all. Hey, Brasi, only imperial boats have purple sails, isn't that right?"

Brasi nodded as he and Noe stepped toward her, forming a circle around her. A circle she could not break.

"You're right," said Aurora, trying to summon the regal bearing of the Empress. The boy with the scar was just a boy, after all. Her mind was probably just confusing memories of long ago. "This is an imperial craft. I was sailing upriver when a storm blew in and carried me downstream and—"

"Is that right?" interrupted Serge, arching one eyebrow, and Aurora could tell that he knew she was lying.

"So, if you can direct me to the palace, I will make sure you receive a handsome reward," she finished, using all her strength to keep her voice calm and steady.

"Really," said Serge. "Why don't we just take you there?"

Aurora heard the friendliness in his tone, but when she looked into his eyes and saw the jagged half-moon below his right eye, memories flashed through her mind. Scary and dark, ugly memories.

"Look!" a voice was saying.

I don't want to look.

"Is that her?"

No, no, it can't be . . . Mama . . . Mama!

"N-No . . . ," Aurora finally stammered, backing away. "No . . ."

She turned and ran, unaware of the yellow parchment that slipped from her pouch and fell to the ground behind her. The chart of the Doors of the Hunab Ku.

"Wait!" called Serge.

She ran without looking back, running as if her life depended on it, away from that scar and a past she didn't want to remember. But it was too late, for she did remember. She could see it so clearly now. The boy named Serge pointing. Her mother's body floating in the water, her long dark hair fanning out around her like a halo, the sunlight glinting off the ring she wore on her left hand. Her wedding ring. It was after the Dragons burned the camp down and took Kareem. Aurora and her mother and Titi had traveled to the city to find Kareem, to beg the Emperor to make them let him go. But their journey had been hopeless, and her mother had died just a few days later.

Aurora ran into the first alley she passed, never noticing the shadow moving behind her in rhythm with her rhythm, in step with her steps.

A shadow figure whose eyes followed her every move, green eyes flecked with black and yellow, cat's eyes like her own.

Niko closed his eyes, waiting for the pain of the blade tearing through his flesh. But it never came.

Instead, he felt the rope give as the sword cut through it, and he fell to the ground.

The cannibal men laughed, just as they had each time they had cut him down in their two days of travel. Each time they stopped they hung him up in a tree by a noose, and laughed in their demonic way, pointing at him and mumbling gibberish Niko couldn't decipher, except for the words *tasty* and *money*. He got the idea, though.

And it made him feel sick to his stomach. They were obviously going to sell him for money or eat him. Either way, he had to get away. He'd tried to work his way out of the net, and he'd try again tonight after they fell asleep. But he doubted he'd have any luck. The dark-haired silent one was a light sleeper and he usually lay down next to Niko.

"I say we sell 'im," said the dark-haired one.

"To who?" asked the leader, bending down and poking Niko with the tip of the silver sword. He raised it higher so that it was at Niko's throat. "I says we should eat 'im."

"I sure is hungry," said red beard. "We ain't had no meat since we killed that rabbit t'other day."

"I bet he'll roast up real good," said the leader, smacking his cracked, bloody lips.

Niko gulped. "Please . . ." The words came out in a whisper. "Don't . . ."

All three of the men laughed again, staring at his stricken face.

"What about the desert divils?" said dark hair, tobacco juice dripping down his chin. "They pay purty good for young boys."

"Mebbe you're right. We could buy us some spirits. Tie 'im up and let's go."

Niko sighed in relief. At least they weren't going to eat him. For now. But who were the desert devils? And how would he ever find Aurora and the charms again?

Red bent down and quickly bound Niko's wrists and ankles with thick rope. Then he picked Niko up and tossed him over his shoulder like a sack of grain. He stepped through the trees after the other two cannibals to where their mangy-looking horses were tethered.

Niko struggled to free himself as he had the day before and the day before that. But Red just laughed, a cold, mirthless sound, and threw him over the back of a horse. There was nothing Niko could do except bide his time.

CHAPTER 13

The dungeon was darker and colder and worse than anything Walker had ever imagined. Much more horrible than the cell he had found himself in earlier. Rats darted in and out of the shadows, and spiders as big as his fist scuttled through the crumbling rocks. Walker picked his steps carefully, holding the torch high as he followed Gibreel along the dark corridor, trying not to notice the cockroaches and the other vermin. But the smell made him gag. Old sweat and human waste and neglect.

"This is disgusting," said Walker, forgetting all

his own aches and pains in the face of this horror. "I've never seen anything so gross in my life."

As usual, Gibreel said nothing as he pulled the food cart along the uneven, rocky floor. Walker stared at the rows of rusty metal doors set into the damp stone.

"What are all these guys in for anyway? Must be pretty bad."

Gibreel shrugged but said nothing. He stopped in front of one door with a small square opening in the middle, took a bowl off the cart, and slid it through the opening carefully so that not a drop of the watery soup spilled. He held the bowl steady as a bruised and scabby hand with long, dirty fingernails reached for it.

"Thank you!" rasped a voice.

Gibreel patted the hand once very gently.

"Bless you, boy," murmured the prisoner.

Walker cringed. How could Gibreel stand to touch someone like that? He followed slowly as the quiet boy pushed the cart to the next cell.

"So how long have you been here?" Walker asked as they rounded a bend in the corridor and descended a ramp to a lower level. "I mean, now that we're alone, you can talk to me, right?"

Gibreel shrugged and kept walking.

"Well, how old were you when you got here?"

Gibreel lifted his shoulders again, dismissing Walker's question.

Walker tried again. "Have you lived your whole life here, or what?"

Gibreel still said nothing, just pushed the cart along. Walker grabbed him by the shoulders and spun him around.

"I need you to talk to me, Gibreel. Why won't you say anything? You help me but refuse to talk? I don't get it."

Gibreel sighed but remained silent, staring down at the floor. Walker grabbed his bony shoulders once more and shook him hard. "What's wrong with you?"

Gibreel looked up very slowly and stared at Walker, his brown eyes deep and sad. And then Gibreel opened his mouth. He had no tongue.

"Oh," Walker gasped, recoiling in shock. "I'm so sorry. I . . . I . . . didn't know."

He was so light-headed, he thought he would faint. He leaned against the wet, crumbling stones and closed his eyes. He felt a gentle pat on his arm, as if in apology, and when he looked up Gibreel stood before him. Gibreel turned then and continued along the narrow corridor, the cart bumping over the rocks behind him.

For the first time in his life, Walker Crane was speechless.

Walker followed Gibreel around a corner into an even narrower passage. There was barely enough room for the two of them to walk single file. At the end of this corridor, they came to a thick door of heavy wood, scarred and nicked with age, locked with three massive iron bolts. Gibreel strained to pull them back, the muscles in his skinny arms bulging. Finally, he opened the door. A steep flight of narrow, winding stairs led down into total darkness.

Someone sure didn't want whoever was down there to get out.

Gibreel took a bowl of soup and pointed down the stairs. Walker led the way, the orange light of his torch bouncing eerily off the old stone walls. At the bottom of the steps was an octagonal room, empty except for a grate in the middle of the floor. Walker watched as Gibreel removed the grate and pulled up a rope with a basket on the end of it. He put the soup in the basket and lowered it down.

Then he motioned for Walker to come.

Walker wondered why, since Gibreel had already fed the prisoner. But he went anyway, and crouched beside him. In the darkness below was a small stone room with a bundle of rags in the corner. Where was the prisoner? Walker wondered if he had escaped. But then the rags began to move and Walker saw that they were actually an old man with long white hair. As he stood, Walker saw that the rags had once been a fine silk robe—the blue material, slashed and torn, hung off his body in jagged strips.

The old man looked up at them, dark eyes in a pale face staring right at Walker.

"So, the Bearer is just a boy. A boy from another world."

Walker's eyes widened and his heart began to beat faster in his chest. How did this old man know he was from another world?

"Listen to me and listen well, Bearer, for there is very little time and I will only say this once:

Black horse rising,
one shall come to ride.
Sign of the Bearer,
the charm by his side.
Nine must be found,
and in the dawning hid.
Nine doors must be opened
or the dark will ne'er be rid.
The dark will rise to take them,
and claim them as their own,
lions in sheep's clothing—
beware or ne'er go home."

When the old man had finished speaking, Walker reached into his pocket, searching for the comforting shape of the red charm. He searched one pocket and then the other, with a growing panic. His pockets were empty.

The charm of fire and blood was gone.

Hours after the sun had set, Walker lay on his cot in the stone dormitory where he'd first met Marcus and company, staring at the black oblong before him, wishing he could somehow crawl through the window and just disappear out of Black Rock forever. So much for his escape plans, now that he had lost the one thing that might have gotten him back to his world and home.

He clenched his fists, thinking longingly of the red charm, the charm of fire and blood. He had hunted for it everywhere—all over the courtyard and up and down the stairs, in the dormitory and the bathrooms. But it was gone. He remembered his mom telling him once when he was very little and had lost his favorite stuffed animal—a lion called Leo, with no eyes and only part of a nose—that sometimes you lost things because you didn't need them anymore.

Walker let his breath out in a long, sad sigh. Not this time. He needed that charm badly. He closed his eyes, thinking of his mother, whom he might never see again. He was so preoccupied with his misery he hadn't noticed the group of boys who had gathered around Marcus at the other end of the room, until Marcus's loud bragging voice forced its way into his thoughts.

"This thing is real valuable," Marcus boasted.

Walker turned his head, still only half listening.

"Yeah," agreed Olan. "It's probably worth a million junos."

"Or even more," said Marcus. "'Cause it's old."

"Let's see it," said another novice.

"Yeah, c'mon, Marcus."

"Hold up, boys," said Marcus. "I'll take it out when I'm good and ready."

Walker sat up, a sick feeling gripping him.

"You can look, but don't touch," ordered Marcus, holding out his hand to reveal Walker's charm.

Walker's breathing quickened as he stared at the charm. His only link to his world. His only hope of escape.

"I bet that thing's worth a billion junos," said Bram.

"You could sell it and live in one of them big houses with servants to bring you cream pudding and tarts and chocolate all day if ya wanted," added Almarine.

"Maybe you should give it to General Da Gama," suggested one boy, not one of Marcus's regular crowd. "I mean, what novice would own something so nice? Maybe it belongs to one of the Dragons or the lord—"

"Shut up, stupid!" said Marcus, glaring at the boy.

"Yeah, jerk-face. Close yer trap." Olan moved closer to the boy, who cowered.

"Wh-What I mean," stammered the boy, "is that if you did that, then you'd probably get lots of points with the Dragons. And I bet they'd let you skip the ceremony of the Five Fires and they'd make you a full-fledged Dragon right away."

"Mebbe," said Marcus. "I'll see what I wanna do."

Walker, with eyes only for the charm, swung his legs over the side of the bed just as the dormitory door opened. Two pages pushed someone into the room and the door once again banged shut. A boy in a torn and muddy green cloak stood before the other novices, shifting uncomfortably from foot to foot. When he saw what Marcus held in his hand, all the color drained from his already pale face.

Walker watched as the boy's light gray eyes rested for a moment on the red charm, almost as if he'd seen it before.

CHAPTER 14

Niko lay quietly, watching the boy in the cot across from him, the one named Marcus. He studied the careless way his arm was flung above his head. The way his gold earring glittered in the moonlight, casting stripes of silver over the bodies of the sleeping boys. He couldn't believe that he had found the lost charm. It *had* worked—it was now in the hands of the Bearer. He was just sorry that he had accused Aurora of losing it. He smiled in the darkness, wishing he could tell her.

He had wanted to speak to Marcus earlier but decided it was better to wait so that no one else would hear. In a few minutes he would wake him up and tell him everything. If only Aurora were here. He sighed, wondering if she'd made it out of the forest, if she and the other charms were safe.

He'd cursed those forest men for capturing him, fought them as hard as he could without a sword, exhausted himself trying to break free, but it had been a waste of energy. Eventually he'd remembered the master's words about situations that appear to be impossible. *Bow to what is.* Accept where you are, for it is where you were meant to be and someday, some way, you will find the right moment to make what you wish come to be.

Niko hadn't wanted to bow, all through the days and nights he'd spent with his captors, especially when they handed him over to the men who had killed his master. But seeing the red charm and Marcus, he'd realized that by not fighting what was, he had come upon exactly what he and Aurora had thought they would never find—the Bearer. He smiled again, feeling oddly close to the master.

Movement near Marcus's cot drew Niko's eye, a shadowy blur beneath the windows. Niko held his breath, watching. As the shadow moved into a patch of moonlight, he saw that it was a boy crawling on all fours. What did he want with the Bearer?

The answer came seconds later when the boy

reached under the Bearer's pillow. The charm! Niko didn't waste a moment. He threw himself on the boy, who was so focused on removing the charm without waking Marcus that he hadn't noticed Niko noticing him. The two wrestled, rolling on the floor.

"Get off me!" shouted Walker.

But Niko wouldn't budge, holding fast to Walker's shoulders so that he couldn't get up.

"I said let me alone!"

"Not until you give back what you took!"

"It's mine!"

Walker kicked at Niko, who had grabbed his right wrist and was trying to pry open his fingers.

The commotion woke some of the boys, including Marcus and Olan.

"What's goin' on?" shouted Olan.

"He took Marcus's—" Niko choked out the words as Walker kneed him hard in the chest.

Marcus, black eyes glinting angrily, jumped on top of both of them, reaching for Walker. "You little snake! Give that back to me!"

"It's mine!" cried Walker, kicking Marcus with his free leg.

"It's mine since I found it."

"I found it first so it belongs to me!"

"Not anymore!"

"That's right, you little worm," agreed Olan, pulling Walker's hair so hard his eyes watered from the pain.

Niko let go his hold on Walker, his thoughts whirling, just as Olan jumped on top of him and kicked him in the stomach. Was Marcus not the Bearer? Could the boy with the yellow hair be the one called by the charm?

Niko watched Marcus punch Walker in the face. The painful blow stunned Walker and he dropped the charm, which rolled across the floor. Olan grabbed it and threw it back to Marcus, who held it in one hand and grinned down at Walker.

"I told you not to mess with me." Marcus nodded at Olan, who grabbed Walker by the arms. "Now you're gonna pay for what you done."

"Give that back!" shouted Walker, his face red, his blue eyes blazing, as he tried to shake the other boy's hold.

Niko knew what he had to do. "Give him the charm," he said.

Marcus looked over at him and snickered, and the other boys laughed with him.

"You gonna make me?"

Niko nodded. "Give. Him. The. Charm."

"Shut your face, new boy," snapped Olan. "Marcus don't gotta listen to you. He don't gotta listen to no one."

"That's right, new boy."

Marcus narrowed his eyes and moved toward Niko. Bram and Olan followed, Walker for the moment forgotten. Niko breathed deeply, feeling the air flow from his abdomen up through his mouth, then exhaled quickly. The empty mind breath for focus. He realized that all his master's teachings that he'd thought applied only to studying and acrobatics also applied to being a warrior. He had just been too blind to see—until now, when it was up to him to save the Bearer—and the charm. He moved his hands beneath the sleeves of his tunic, through the series of focusing exercises he had been taught before his balancing exercises.

"Scared to fight, are you?" taunted Marcus as Olan pulled a knife out of his pocket.

Niko did not allow his eyes to linger on Marcus or the knife Olan thrust forward. He could hear Lord Amber's words echoing in his head as clearly as if the two of them were sitting together in the library and the master was instructing him how to concentrate to solve a complex problem of logic. *When the breath wanders, the mind is unsteady, but when the breath is still, so is the mind.*

Niko continued to breathe air in slowly, forcing it out fast with his diaphragm, and watched Bram and Olan and a tall, pale-eyed boy who had joined the circle, without tilting his head in the slightest, his eyes shifting right and left, making an almost 180-degree turn to each side. He noticed without appearing to see that Marcus had avoided putting any weight on his left foot.

Olan started the fight with a lunge of his knife. In that fraction of a second, Niko could hear his master's words floating through the air toward him, as if he were there in the moonlit room too. *When you see with your heart, you have found right mind, and that is where right action comes from.*

Niko leaped up, tucking his left leg beneath him and extending his right leg. Then in midair, his left leg shot out at Marcus with the swiftness and strength of a leopard, hitting his left hand with so much force that it knocked the charm to the floor.

Walker and Bram lunged for the charm as Olan jumped at Niko with the knife.

Then you cannot fail, for you have found a path with heart. The words ran through Niko's mind like the ocean breaking against the castle rocks, smoothly, ceaselessly, eternally.

Olan thrust the knife at Niko, who stepped to the

side just as Marcus swung toward him. Marcus and Olan collided and the knife caught Marcus in the shoulder. Olan stared at the blood in horror.

"Get 'im!" cried the other boys. "Get the new boy!"

Bram looked up at the commotion, and Walker knocked him out of the way, seizing the charm. Niko's and Walker's eyes locked as footsteps sounded in the hall. Now what? Walker wondered. They had to get out of there. Like magic, Gibreel appeared at his side and grabbed Walker's sleeve, motioning him toward the bathroom. Walker nodded at Niko and the two of them sprinted down the row of cots to the door at the far end.

"They're running away!" shouted Almarine just as the dormitory door banged open.

Gibreel headed for the third stall, opened the wooden door, and pulled out the same rock behind which he had hidden Walker's sneakers. He handed the shoes to Walker and then stepped back, motioning for them to crawl into the hole. Footsteps sounded on the stone floor of the bathroom, just feet away.

"They're in the stall!" cried a voice.

There were muffled shouts and the clacking of the Dragons' boots on the tiled floor.

"C'mon!" urged Walker, climbing into the hole.

Niko clambered after him, and then they were plunged in darkness as the rock was replaced, blocking out the light and the sound.

"Gibreel!" Walker pounded on the stone, but it wouldn't budge.

"He's not coming," Niko said.

"I hope he's all right."

"There's nothing we can do about it now."

Walker didn't say anything. He thought of the red stump where Gibreel's tongue should have been and he shuddered. Please, be okay, he thought, the closest he could get to a prayer.

Just up ahead the tunnel forked in two directions.

"Let's go this way," said Niko, pointing to the left.

"I think we should go right," insisted Walker. "You're always supposed to turn clockwise, like if you're lost in a forest or something."

Niko shook his head. "See how the darkness looks a little lighter to the left? Where light gets in, maybe we can get out. At least that's how it is in my castle."

"Your castle?"

"The Castle of the Seven Towers, where I come from."

"Oh," said Walker, not knowing what else to say. This world was far different from his.

"Follow me."

Walker shrugged and crawled after him. It was dark and damp in the tunnel. Loose rocks dug into his hands and knees. They heard an occasional squeaking, which Walker was sure meant rats. He tried not to think about it.

"So where did you learn to fight like that?" he asked instead.

"My master taught me." Niko sighed in the darkness, wishing he could tell Lord Amber that he finally understood what he meant about being a warrior of the pen and of the sword. But, of course, it was too late for that.

"Master?"

"He was training me."

"How do you know about the charm?"

"You mean charms."

"There's more than one?"

"There're nine. Don't you know the rhyme?"

Walker said he didn't, so Niko recited it for him. "I'm the Chooser. The one who chose the red charm that brought you through to this world. My name's Niko."

"Where's the Protector?"

"She's . . . well . . . I'm not sure, but she has the other charms—at least, I hope so."

"That's just great," said Walker with a sigh. "I'm never going to get home at this rate."

"Home?"

"Yeah, home. Back to my world. Unless you know how to send me."

"All I know is what's in the rhyme, which means, I think, that one day you'll become the first new Lord of Time."

"Lord of Time? Me?"

"I guess so. But I don't think it's as simple as all that. I think you have to pass a test. Maybe we all have to pass a test and help win the war."

"What war?"

"The one between the light and the dark." That was all Niko said because it was all he knew about the war. He wasn't even sure whether it had started yet. Unless the Dragons killing Lord Amber was the first move by the dark and he and Aurora finding the charms and bringing the Bearer through was the first move by the light. This was nothing like the War of the Flowers between the kingdoms of Sunnebēam and Kasmania, because that was all about territory. This, well, this was about—what did the rhyme say? "Taking back the night."

"What side are we on?"

Walker's question brought Niko back to the moment. "The light, of course."

Light, thought Walker. Miss Hamilton and the haystacks popped into his mind.

"You know what? I don't want to be a Lord of Time. I just want to go back to L.A. The sun shines all the time there and I live with my mom and my brother and my dog, Blue. And—what does it matter? I'm never gonna get back there."

Niko didn't say anything. He had nowhere to return to now that Lord Amber was gone. But of course Walker couldn't know that. They crawled in silence until the tunnel ended at a stone wall.

"Now what?" said Walker.

He watched as Niko slipped his fingers over the rocks in front of them, feeling for something.

"What are you doing?"

Niko didn't answer. His pale forehead furrowed as he frowned in concentration. He began to press on one big rock in the bottom center of the wall. He turned and motioned for Walker to push.

"What is this? Another secret passage?"

"It seems to be."

"How do you know?"

"My master taught me that in the dark there is light, just as in the light there is dark. You cannot have one without the other. It is one of the immutable laws."

"What does that have to do with finding a secret passage?"

"When I count to three, push."

Walker shook his head, but when Niko threw all his weight against the rock, he did too. Slowly the rock began to roll forward. They pushed again and again, the rock each time moving just a fraction.

"We'll never move it," whispered Walker in frustration.

"Imagine that it has moved and that you see the space beyond. When you push, think of that space. It will help move the rock."

"Give me a break," said Walker. "Just thinking something has nothing to do with actually doing it."

"Suit yourself," said Niko.

They pushed again and this time Walker thought of how strange his new companion was. Visualizing empty space was crazy. A picture of the empty passage beyond the rock popped into his mind nevertheless. And the next thing he knew, the rock rolled back far enough for the two of them to squeeze through.

Walker shook his head in surprise, about to say something, when both boys froze. Behind them they heard thudding, faint but unmistakable.

"Dragons," whispered Walker.

Quickly they rolled the rock back into place on the other side. Then they began to crawl through an even narrower passage, so tight that Walker could feel the stones, wet with moisture and furry with mildew, brushing him on both sides. It reminded him of a drainpipe. A few moments later he realized it *was* a drain when the passage suddenly sloped down and they both slid into a pool of cold water. Their heads slammed into a square metal grating that trapped them in a small chamber with barely enough room for the two of them to sit side by side.

"Where are we?"

"I don't know. I can't see anything," said Niko, peering up through the grating, the darkness pressing on his eyeballs.

"How are we going to get out of here?"

Niko reached up and ran his fingers over the metal. He could feel the jagged outline of a bolt. As he pulled, it loosened and he was able to undo it. He felt for another bolt and loosened it, too, until he could lift up the grating. He hoisted himself up through the opening and Walker followed. They found themselves in a long, low-ceilinged room with a pool in the center dimly lit by candles in covered sconces on the walls. Clouds of steam rose from the pool, filling the place with swirling mist. Walker began to sweat at once, and the thick, humid air filled his lungs so that he coughed.

"I think the door's over there," whispered Niko, pointing to the opposite side of the pool, where the mist hung thick and white so that Walker couldn't make out a thing.

"How can you tell?"

Niko shrugged. "It's the logical place for a door in a room like this, if you consider the golden mean."

"Golden what? Oh, forget it. Sounds like geometry or something I don't want to know."

Niko motioned Walker forward, and they stepped carefully so as not to slip on the slick tiles. The air in the room was so hazy from the steam, Walker could barely see Niko's back in front of him. They both froze when they heard the murmur of voices and the slam of a door. A draft of cool air blew into the room and they ducked behind a stone ledge.

"And how is the Emperor?" asked a voice Walker remembered only too well.

"All will be done in a matter of hours, the doctors say. A day at most."

"And the box?"

The other man began to speak, but his voice was so low Walker couldn't make out another word he said.

"Speak up, Mouse! It is only the two of us. You do not have to worry about imperial spies here."

The lord laughed then and the spy called Mouse

laughed with him, but not with any heart. Walker and Niko turned to each other. If they were caught, they would die.

"I pulled the paper out of the box, like you said."

"Good. And whose name was it?"

"Lord Amber."

Walker felt Niko stiffen beside him.

"And you replaced the name as you were instructed?"

Mouse must have nodded because the lord said, "Good. And now for your reward."

Walker raised his head to see what the lord was doing, but only caught a glimpse of his red robe.

"You know what they say when two men have a secret, Mouse?"

There was a gasping sound and a thud.

"That it's only safe with one."

Walker and Niko stared at each other, hearts pounding.

"For the new order to be ushered in, the old order must die. Over and over, endlessly beginning and ending, through time and space, until now, when the Nine Doors of the Hunab Ku are opened and the charms returned to the place from which they came." The lord's words resonated in the misty room, cut short by the sound of a door closing.

Walker puzzled over the lord's words, for they

sounded oddly familiar. The nine doors! They were part of the poem the old man in the dungeon had told him. *Nine doors must be opened.*

"Let's go," whispered Niko after a few more minutes.

Silently they tiptoed across the room. Walker tripped, stopping short and staring in horror at the body he had almost stepped on. Through the mist that swirled all around them, he could see blood—and something long and thin that looked like a string around the man's neck.

"Ohmygod," he gasped. "Ohmygod."

"C'mon," said Niko. "We'd better go."

Walker nodded, knowing Niko was right. There was nothing they could do for this man, and if they didn't hurry, they would end up just like him. But how, Walker wondered, had the lord killed a man in seconds with only a string?

He decided he didn't want to know.

Across the room, they found a door just where Niko had said it would be. They slipped through it into a dark hallway and ran. Down that hall, through various rooms, finally coming to a metal door, which Walker realized at once was the same one the Dragon guards had pushed him through when they brought him from the dungeon to General Da Gama.

He fumbled at the latch and they hurried through, closing the door quietly behind them, into the same sandy courtyard where General Da Gama had punished Walker in front of all the boys. The gates loomed tall before them, the desert and freedom lying just beyond.

Niko made as if to head for the gates, but Walker stopped him.

"This way," Walker called. He headed around the corner onto the cobblestones of another courtyard. He was pretty sure the stables were just across this courtyard, in the long, low building beyond. There were no Dragons or pages in sight, so he led the way toward it, wondering uneasily why it was so quiet.

In that instant they heard the rasping of metal as a door opened somewhere behind them.

"There they are!" came a voice.

"Heading for the stables!" called another.

Walker and Niko both looked back, saw the torches and the red robes approaching, and broke into a run. With the Dragons just yards away, Walker tried to open the barn's double doors, but his fingers slipped. If he got caught this time, General Da Gama would have no mercy. The fear made him clumsy. The latch slipped again, and Walker stepped back cursing as Niko reached for the iron bar and pulled it free. They flew down the long central aisle of the barn, the horses pacing in their stalls, nickering at the sudden commotion.

Niko opened a stall door and led out a large bay colored stallion. Quickly he swung up and mounted.

"Hurry!" he shouted. "They're coming!"

But Walker continued down the aisle. He knew she had to be here, but somewhere apart where her wildness wouldn't disrupt the other horses. He turned up the next aisle, searching still.

Niko rode up behind him, his face pale in the moonlight. "What are you doing? Just take any horse."

Running footsteps and the muffled shouts of the Dragons outside filtered into the dark stable.

As if he hadn't heard, Walker moved on, his eyes quickly scanning the horses. Without the incredible speed of the Black Asha on their side, they might never make it to freedom. There was a crashing as the stable doors were flung open, and Walker's heart, already beating wildly in his chest, began to thump even harder.

Where was she? He kept searching, running down the next aisle, his eyes roaming the stalls. Down another aisle and there it was. Like an answer to a prayer, he found her, finally. One stall set apart from the others with no window. From behind the door, he could hear the thumping of hooves and fiery snorting and he knew she was there.

The Black Asha. Waiting for him.

He drew the heavy bolts and flung open the door. The wild black horse flashed her dark eyes, and pawed the straw uneasily, nostrils flaring, ears set back.

Walker moved slowly toward the horse, staring into her eyes, making soft, soothing sounds with his tongue. "Hey, girl. Remember me?"

"We have to get out of here," urged Niko.

"Go. I'll catch up," Walker said without turning.

Slowly he stretched out one hand, running it over the sleek black hair of her mane. "Good girl," he whispered.

She whinnied and snorted, but Walker didn't back away. He kept talking to her and stroking her mane, the way he used to calm his dog during a storm. The Black Asha began to quiet, her eyes never leaving Walker's face. Slowly he led her out of the stall and down the aisle in a different direction than the one they'd come from. Somewhere behind them, just a few aisles away, the Dragons threw open stall doors, searching for them, and the disturbed horses whinnied and stamped their feet.

"Come on," Niko urged as he rode toward the rear door.

Walker didn't say anything. He just concentrated on leading the Black Asha, who stopped every few yards and pawed the ground. He didn't want to mount her in the barn for fear of scaring her even more.

She snorted suddenly and came to a dead stop. Over and over in his mind, Walker urged the horse to be calm and walk out. The Dragons would find them any moment, if they didn't hurry. As if she could hear him, the Black Asha began to walk once more. Relieved, Walker hurried forward. They were almost there. But then the shouts of the Dragons echoed through the stables, and she began to neigh and buck.

Only a few yards to go. "Come on, horse," he pleaded. The door was just in sight.

Then they were there. He grabbed her mane and pulled himself up onto her back. It was like sitting on top of a house, she was so big.

"C'mon, girl," urged Walker, but the massive animal would not budge. Her ears flicked back and forth.

"They're at the back!" cried a voice as a Dragon appeared in the aisle behind him, like a devil lit by the orange flame of his torch.

The shout of the Dragon seemed to awaken something in the horse and before Walker knew what had happened, the Black Asha tore through the doorway into the courtyard. He had to hold on tightly so he wouldn't fall off, the cold night wind making his tunic billow like a sail. Riding the Black Asha was nothing like a pony ride. Too bad he'd never taken riding lessons.

Behind him he could see the torches flickering as the Dragons raced toward them. He urged the Black Asha to catch up with Niko, who was somewhere around the corner, out of view. He raced around the turn, and what he saw almost made him give up right then and there. Lining the tower wall that encircled the House of the Black Rock stood a hundred Dragons, bows and arrows in their hands. Arrows whizzed through the air. Walker watched in horror as Niko's horse stumbled and fell, blood oozing from a wound in her side. Niko sprawled on the ground, the arrows flying all around him.

"Niko, I'm coming!" Walker whispered. The Black Asha galloped into the melee as if she had read his mind, heading right for Niko, who had just stumbled to his feet.

"There's the other one!" cried a voice as another volley of arrows was unleashed. Walker could feel the arrows whizzing through the air around him like hail falling during an ice storm, but he and the Black Asha rode on impervious, the eyes of the boy and the beast only for Niko.

The Black Asha slowed for a moment, and Walker hoisted Niko up behind him. He kicked into the Black Asha's sides as the old man's voice echoed in his head: *"Black horse rising, one shall come to ride. Sign of the Bearer, the charm by his side."*

The Black Asha raced across the moonlit courtyard toward the tall gates, which Walker noted in surprise were partly open. As they drew closer, the volley of arrows stopped. Before he could wonder why, Walker saw the reason. Some men on horseback were trotting through the gates away from Black Rock with a cart tied behind them.

An image of the dead man named Mouse popped into Walker's mind. And he wondered, with a sickening feeling in the pit of his stomach, if he was in the cart.

As the last man rode through, the gates began to shut.

"Hurry!" he urged, kicking into the Black Asha's sides once more.

"Close the gate!" shouted a Dragon as more arrows were unleashed, whizzing through the air above their heads.

The thundering of hooves echoed through the

courtyard as Dragons on horseback charged after them.

"The gate!" cried Niko as the heavy wooden doors swung toward each other.

"Fly!" shouted Walker, leaning over the Black Asha's neck.

She hesitated for a moment as Dragons swarmed from every direction. Walker closed his eyes, ready for the impact. But just as the gates inched their way closer together, the Black Asha jumped through the diminishing gap. The gates thudded shut behind them and they could hear the angry shouts of the Dragons as they hit the solid wooden barrier.

Walker and Niko rode away from the House of the Black Rock and into the desert night.

CHAPTER 15

Aurora crouched in the shadows opposite the doorway of the large sitting room. She had chosen this spot behind a tall cabinet made of shiny dark wood because it gave her the advantage of being able to see whoever entered the room without being seen herself. She longed to stand and stretch her legs, but she was afraid some servant or imperial guard might catch sight of her. She hadn't come all this way to risk discovery now. So she stayed still where she was, waiting.

She stared about the room, from the draperies hung with gold and precious stones, to the vases filled with flowers, to the shimmering crystal that lined the shelves of the gold-leaf cabinet across from her. I hope this is right, she thought. Worse than any pain was the worry that she hadn't overheard the guards correctly about the Empress's wing of the palace. But nowhere else had she seen so many flowers, tulips especially. And this was the only door she had found that was made of ivory with a solid gold handle embossed with golden tulips.

The golden doorknob began to turn. Aurora was surprised, as she hadn't heard approaching footsteps, more surprised still when she saw who slipped into the room, closing the door softly behind. Castor Le Croix looked about him as if searching for something. His gaze rested for a moment on the cabinet behind which Aurora hid, making her feel very exposed. But his gaze passed beyond the cabinet. And then just as quickly returned, a frown creasing his forehead.

Aurora watched in horror as Castor began to walk toward her. He stopped in front of her hiding place, just inches from where she crouched. She held her breath. His eyes traveled to the top of the cabinet. Please, don't look over the edge, she chanted in her mind. Don't look over the edge. She clenched her fist so hard the fingernails dug into the skin. Don't look over the edge.

He didn't. He stared instead at the crystal bottles arranged on a piece of white silk that lined the top of the cabinet. She watched him choose a flask filled with purple liquid. He slipped a piece of folded white paper out of his pocket and opened it over the bottle, releasing a white powder, which he swirled around in the bottle until it disappeared. As he reached down to replace the paper in the pocket of his yellow robe, she caught a glimpse of a symbol stamped at the top. It was of five monkeys in a row.

She'd seen those monkeys, but before she could think of where, the door opened once again and the Empress glided into the room. She wore the same circlet of rubies and diamonds pulling back her long dark hair, and the same jeweled slippers on her feet. But she was different. It was not a physical difference, but more to do with her attitude and bearing, a quiet, empty calm, a kind of giving up or giving in, Aurora wasn't sure which.

"Your Majesty . . . cousin . . . I have been looking for you," Castor purred. He smiled and bowed low as the Empress slid onto a striped couch across from Aurora.

"You know that I worry about you, cousin, especially with the Emperor so far gone. We all know it won't be long now, however distressing that thought may be."

The Empress stared at Castor with an empty look in her beautiful almond-shaped eyes but said nothing.

"Something to clear your head?" Castor asked.

Without waiting for a reply, he moved toward the cabinet, picked up the bottle with the purple liquid, and poured some into a glass. Aurora's mind raced. She watched as he calmly walked over to the Empress, the poisoned drink in his hand. The Empress reached for the glass with a small smile on her lips.

"Your father and I were only trying to do the best for you," said Castor, his voice harder now, as the Empress raised the glass. "But you never understood. I see that now. You could think only of yourself, your happiness, instead of the happiness of the many. One day Kasmania will rise, for I will never forget the vow I made to your father, the—"

Aurora didn't waste another second. She charged out of her hiding place and hurled herself at the Empress. She managed to knock the glass to the floor just before the Empress raised it to her lips.

"He's trying to kill you," Aurora choked out, staring up into the Empress's face for the first time, into those almond-shaped eyes. And what she saw instead of a flicker of recognition was a silvery green sparkle of light.

"Beware others like me . . ." Calliope's words echoed in Aurora's mind.

She stumbled to her feet. This wasn't the Empress at all, but one of the Sisters of the Kuxan-Sunn. So where was the real Empress? And why would the Sisters kidnap her? Aurora wondered in a panic.

"Aurora is your name, is it not?" questioned Castor, pointing a small pearl-handled weapon at her face. "And besides being a thief, it appears that you are also a liar, two qualities that I have found often go hand in hand in the lower order of beings."

"I . . . I . . . don't know what you're talking about," Aurora sputtered, backing away from Castor.

Castor Le Croix pressed something on the weapon and it clicked. Aurora tried to swallow the lump that rose in her throat.

"Your Majesty, I'm afraid this girl has stolen a very important imperial document. One which I believe you know very well. The punishment for which, I believe, is hanging, is it not?"

The Empress who was not the Empress didn't answer, her eyes as empty as the shattered crystal on the floor. Aurora realized as she stared from her to Castor that Le Croix didn't know that the spirit posing before him was not of human blood. So the

Sisters weren't working with him. Did they want the chart and the charms for themselves? Or were they working with someone else? The Dragons? But that didn't make sense if the Dragons were working for Castor—and Kasmania. Unless someone was double-crossing someone else.

"How do you feel about hanging, Aurora? The citizens of Sunnebēam all gathered to watch as the box is knocked from beneath you and the cord tightens round your neck."

Before Castor had finished his sentence, the castle bells began to ring, the tones echoing so loudly they seemed to shake the very stones of the room. A moment later three imperial guards rushed in, all dressed in the imperial purple and white.

"It is the Emperor, Your Majesty," a guard said, and bowed. "He has drawn his last breath."

In the chaos that followed, Aurora slipped out of the room. She could hear Castor's voice behind her, shouting, "Stop the thief!" but he was drowned out by the steady tolling of the bells, the pounding of footsteps, and the echoing cries of the royal family and the palace staff as the mourning began.

Aurora ran down the hallway, intent on evading Castor and the guards, but wondering too where the Empress was. That must have been what her dream was about, what Calliope had meant when she told

Aurora to follow her dreams. It was up to Aurora to save the Empress. She just hoped she wasn't too late. She was thinking so hard that she didn't see the huge crowd before her, bodies jostling, elbowing each other, as they surged toward the golden double doors at the end of the hall.

Aurora turned back, but the crowd grew behind her too. She had no choice but to go along with the pushing, shoving crowd, all moving toward those golden doors.

She quickly found herself in a massive stone room, thronged with people, all gathered around a bed hung with white drapery.

Aurora stared at the bed. She had seen it before in the Empress's mind. That was where she had seen Castor Le Croix's five monkeys, too. All signs for her to follow, but what did they mean? She didn't know.

A hush descended on the crowd as a door just behind the bed opened. Into the room came an older, thickset man dressed in purple robes. Behind him was the Empress, or rather the Sister in disguise.

"We have gathered here to mourn the passing of Emperor Kristo the Second. His son, Valentine Justas, shall one day take up his mantle. But until the child becomes a man, a regent will rule Sunnebēam and supervise the training of our young Emperor."

The fat man nodded, and one of the guards appeared and handed him a small wooden box.

"The name of the regent, chosen by the Emperor before his death, is in this box. Empress, shall you do us the honor?"

The box, Aurora thought, watching the Sister Empress reach for it, holding it lightly in her jeweled fingers. The box. The Emperor mentioned a box in the note to Lord Amber. The Emperor had been afraid of something going wrong with the box. Aurora put the pieces together all of a sudden. And that was why he had written to Lord Amber. He was afraid someone would tamper with the box. The dark.

The crowd watched expectantly as the Sister Empress withdrew a small slip of folded white paper.

"And who shall be the regent of the kingdom of Sunnebēam, decreed by his holiness Emperor Kristo the Second?"

The silent anticipation hummed in Aurora's ears.

"Lord Draco, now the Grand High," murmured the Empress in a soft but distinct voice.

Not a word, not a murmur, greeted the announcement. Aurora looked at the stricken faces around her. She had never heard of Lord Draco. Was he, could he be, the dark one whom the Emperor feared?

"The kingdom of Kasmania supports the new regent," announced a cold voice that penetrated even the corners of the silent room. Castor Le Croix stood off to one side, not far from the bed where the dead Emperor lay.

The official smiled at the ambassador as if pleased. And Aurora knew in that instant that Castor Le Croix was working with this Lord Draco to take over the kingdom. But how did the Sisters fit in? So many layers of deceit and intrigue, Aurora thought. How will I know what to do or who to trust?

The Empress turned as if to leave as one voice rose above the murmurs of the crowd. One crying voice, wailing mournfully not far from Aurora. "God help us if the dark one is come."

And then the whole room burst into noise, sobbing, screaming, pushing, shoving, voices calling for order. Castor Le Croix turned toward the voice, and in that moment, Aurora met the gaze of his one light-blue eye. He moved toward her, shoving people aside.

She pushed and elbowed to the back of the room. She was small, which helped her slip through the surging crowd. She fought her way out of the room and ran down one marble corridor after another, finally slowing to catch her breath. She was looking around, trying to get her bearings, when she was grabbed suddenly from behind. A hand covered her mouth.

"At last," murmured a voice.

Aurora struggled, twisting and kicking, unable to believe that Castor Le Croix had somehow managed to slip through the crowds and catch her after all. But he held her fast, and when she finally found herself face-to-face with him, she gasped. It wasn't Castor Le Croix at all, but the Dragon called Jah.

Aurora stared into those green-and-yellow eyes and in that instant knew them. Those same eyes had stared defiantly up at the Dragon who'd been about to kill her so long ago. She could see a little boy holding tightly to her white dagger, thrusting it toward the Dragon, yelling at her to run. But she hadn't run. She had stayed where she was, waiting for her brother, Kareem, to run with her.

But he had not escaped with her. He had been taken away by the Dragon into the night. And the white dagger was all she had left to remember him by. The white dagger that this same Dragon had taken from her just days before. The same white dagger that had so mesmerized him that he had let Niko and Aurora get away.

"No," gasped Aurora, staring into those cold eyes. "No." But she knew, as surely as she knew her own name.

The Dragon, face impassive, eyes unreadable, twisted her arms behind her back and tied her wrists.

"Kareem!" she cried.

But the Dragon named Jah refused to look at her, refused to hear as she repeated his name over and over, "Kareem! Kareem!" And then, "It's me, your sister, Aurora!"

He simply bound her mouth so that she could no longer speak, and she was forced to swallow all her words of love and pain and loss as she stared at the brother whom she'd dreamed of finding for so long. Be careful of what you wish for, she thought too late.

CHAPTER 16

The Black Asha stood by a small rock formation, rising up out of the desert like a lonely monument surrounded by sand. She stared into the distance. The wind was picking up, shrieking across the flat desert expanse, whipping the sand in frenzied rivulets, churning it, sending it flying in every direction. She lifted her foot out of the swirling sand and cried out once.

Walker, asleep on her back, slipped off and fell to the roiling ground. He woke immediately, spitting sand out of his mouth, staring into the raging storm. The Black Asha's legs were already buried. He looked around and saw that Niko had also fallen off but was still sleeping, exhausted by their hours of riding from one night into the next. Walker saw in horror that he was already half covered by sand.

"Niko!" he shouted into the wind, his words snatched out of his mouth and blown away into the darkness. "Niko, get up!"

But Niko didn't move. Sand blew into Walker's face, making it hard to see and hard to breathe. He began to panic as the sand covered him, too. He scrambled to his feet, taking one step toward Niko, but the force of the wind was so strong, it blew him away from Niko and the horse. Too late he saw that the Black Asha had positioned them behind the rocks to protect them from the blowing sand.

Now Walker faced the full fury of the storm.

He gritted his teeth and tried to move back to the rocks. But once more he was blown even farther away. The sand came so fast he was afraid he would be buried if he didn't keep moving.

An eerie whistling insinuated itself in the howl of blowing wind. Walker stared into the horizon, wondering what further horror awaited him. Dimly he made out a shape gliding toward him, wrapped in a field of calm. As the figure drew closer to Walker, the sand stopped blowing, as if held at bay by the figure's will, although around and beyond the storm raged on. Walker blinked, wiping sand out of his eyes, staring at the strange apparition before him. Wearing a long blue-green dress that shimmered like fish's scales, now silver, now blue, now green, now gold, face hidden behind a veil, the figure floated over the sand.

More figures followed the first, differing only in size. Like blue-green angels without wings, the figures floated closer, singing a strange song. With them came a calm untouched by the fury of the sandstorm.

"Ssomnus ssspiritus sssanctusss." The chorus of gentle voices sang the strange words in a whisper.

There was something about those sibilant voices that bothered him. Walker didn't know what. Couldn't think. Their voices were so soothing, like a lullaby, making his mind swim.

He watched transfixed as they raised their arms above their heads, drawing closer and closer. The hair beneath their veils was long and golden and their eyes a deep bright blue. He tried to rise, but his head felt so heavy, all he could do was lift it a few inches.

One of the creatures stood by his feet. She was not singing like the others. She was staring at him. He tried to look away, but her eyes held his gaze like a magnet. He forgot for a minute about the sandstorm and Niko and the Dragons. The creature smiled a slow, inviting smile, and he couldn't help it. He smiled back.

As the others finished their song, they clustered around him, forming a ring. They looked as if they were made of air and wind and light—translucent, changeable like the dawn and the sea. He stared at them, unafraid, soothed by their presence.

The one by his feet lowered her hands and began to speak in a soft, gentle whisper. "We know you want to go home. To wake up from this nightmare. That is why we have come. There is only one thing you mussst do."

Walker listened hard. Home, he thought wistfully. "I want to go home," he told them.

"All you have to do isss reach into your pocket," hissed Ijada, eldest Sister of the Kuxan-Sunn. "Reach deep into your pocket."

Walker could not resist. He wanted to please this beautiful creature. He slipped his hand into his pocket. His fingers slid over the cold, smooth shape of the charm.

"Very good," came Ijada's singsong voice. "Now show usss the charm."

Slowly Walker pulled out the charm he had fought so hard to protect, the charm he had almost died for. He held it in his hand.

Ijada's eyes sparkled so brightly, a trail of blue sparks flashed into the shadows. She smiled at Walker, and his pleasure at her happiness was almost a physical thing.

"The nightmare is almossst over, Walker," she whispered, her voice gentle and reassuring.

"Yes," piped up the smallest creature, who floated right next to Walker and then knelt beside him. She lifted her veil and threw it over her head so that her golden hair tumbled over her shoulders. She leaned toward him until her face was just inches from his. Walker stared into her eyes, entranced by her breath on his cheek. He closed his eyes, anticipating her kiss, but instead she whispered, "Soon you'll be home with your dog. Blue misses you so much."

"Jussst place the charm in my hand and repeat after me," crooned Ijada, floating closer. "I give you, the Sisters of the Kuxan-Sunn, Guardians of the Pathways, the first charm, willingly and without remorse, with all my heart and all my soul."

Walker stretched out his hand, palm up. Could it really be true, he wondered, that all he had to do to get back home was to give this strange creature the charm and say a few words? He smiled in anticipation, the charm glowing with its ruby-red light in the darkness, like a beacon, like a star, as the Sisters stared at it hungrily. Ijada stretched out one shimmering green-and-silver-clad arm for the red charm. But her need for the charm scared Walker, and he jerked his hand back. The littlest one frowned, her lips curling into a pout as she recoiled from him.

"Look!" crooned Ijada. "There is someone here from your world who wants to ssspeak to you."

A woman in a long yellow dress floated just beyond the circle of Sisters. She smiled at Walker and waved.

"Walker, come home!" she called.

"Mom!" screamed Walker. "Mom!"

But she didn't move toward him. It was as if she couldn't hear him.

"We miss you so much," said his mother softly. "Just do what the Sisters ask, Walker. Give them the charm. And then we'll all be together again."

"I miss you, Mom." Walker sighed.

The image of Walker's mother began to fade and her voice grew fainter until it was barely there, like the whisper of wind in leaves. "Come home, Walker. Please, come home." Her voice echoed in his head. "Just give up the charm and come home."

Walker stretched out his hand and Ijada leaned toward him once more, reaching for the charm, ready to claim its glowing magnificence, when suddenly the Black Asha cried out, pawing the ground. The wild black horse began to run to Walker, fighting the wind and sand. Walker gasped as he remembered where he had heard the singsong voice before. He pulled his hand back and bolted up, his self-control finally returning, remembering the conversation between the Sister named Ijada and the lord, conscious now of what he had almost done, clutching the charm tightly.

"No!" he cried, shaking his fist at the Sisters as the charm burned its light into his skin and gave him strength. "Go away and leave me alone!"

The Sisters recoiled at his words, their blue eyes rimmed with fiery red. The littlest one reached toward him as if to snatch the charm out of his hand.

"Don't!" shouted Ijada. "He mussst give it willingly, or we will all perish."

The littlest sister pulled back her hand and glared at Walker. "Give it to us." She hurled the words like knives. "Give it to us or you'll be trapped here forever with no way home."

Walker hesitated and then glared back at her. "No!" The prisoner's strange words floated to him as if the old man were there somehow, warning him. *The dark will rise to take them, and claim them as their own, lions in sheep's clothing—beware or ne'er go home.* Lions in sheep's clothing. Evil masquerading as good, the vicious as the gentle.

"I would die before I ever gave up this charm."

The wind picked up as the Sisters began to float away from him. Their departure brought back the storm with all its wild, violent ragings. Sand swirled through the air, into Walker's eyes and nose, blinding him, making it almost impossible to breathe.

"You'll be sorry," hissed the littlest Sister. "For I will be watching you day after day and night after night. And when you slip, I will be there. You will beg me to take the charm so that I can spare you your pain. But I will not help you."

"No!" shouted Walker, spitting out a mouthful of sand. "No!"

He couldn't tell whether the Sisters heard him. He could barely see as their shimmering shadows disappeared into the storm.

Desperation clutched Walker as the sand whirled ceaselessly around him, covering him so fast that he could no longer see his legs. He had to find Niko and get out of the blowing wind. He crawled, squeezing his eyes shut against the blowing sand, moving, he hoped, in the right direction. The wind blew so hard that he could barely keep himself on all fours, so he lowered himself onto his belly and slid like a snake, inch by inch. After each tiny move forward, he had to lower his head to the ground to catch his breath, and then try again.

Finally his fingers felt something hard. The edge

of the rocks. Walker pulled himself into the hollow, thankful that he had made it there alive, and there was Niko, sitting up, leaning against the rocks. But his eyes were glassy and dazed, oblivious of the sand that covered him up to his head like a blanket.

"Niko!" cried Walker.

But he didn't answer.

"Niko! It's me!"

The silver eyes registered no recognition. Niko's hands made no motions to clear the sand that was burying him alive. Walker scrambled forward and tried to brush the sand off Niko, but more sand blew to cover him as fast as Walker could clear it. He realized in that moment that all he did was for nothing because the storm was going to kill them.

He sank down beside his new friend and waited. At least it won't take long to die, he thought.

At first he thought it was just a trick of his desperate eyes. But then he saw that it was a ring of lights floating in the air, which, when it turned on its side, looked like a hoop of fire he'd once seen at the circus. Through the sphere of light, Walker saw in surprise, the sand did not blow.

He struggled to his feet, pulling Niko up beside him. The two stood, leaning against each other, bracing themselves against the wind.

"Come on, Niko," cried Walker, pulling him toward the ring of lights.

Niko, unresponsive, allowed Walker to drag him. One step. Another step. It was hard going, with the wind fiercely pushing them backward and Niko like dead weight in his arms.

"Just a little farther," Walker yelled as the wind wailed all around them. A sense of urgency filled him. They had to get there now before the lights disappeared.

They were almost there. One more step. A gust of wind took Walker's breath, and then the Black Asha snorted, tossing her mane wildly. As Walker took the first step through the sphere of lights, the Asha was right behind him, pushing Niko forward with her great black head.

Walker stopped to catch his breath. He and Niko stood side by side on a dry, dusty mountain ledge. Above them the sun shone. All around towered red sandstone mountains. But best of all, not a breath of air was stirring. There was no wind.

Walker turned behind him, looking for the Black Asha. But she was gone. All that was left was the shimmering ring of lights. He and Niko were alone in a new world.

CHAPTER 17

A cold wind swept across the empty desert sands, sending a chill that cut through Aurora's thin cotton dress. She barely felt it as she stared at the ramrod-straight back of the Dragon who rode before her. He was taking her to the Dragons at the House of the Black Rock. The charms were in his possession. She had failed so miserably she might as well die, just close her eyes and disappear along with her brother, Kareem. She had lost so much. The charms, the Chooser, the Empress, her grandmother, and her home. And worst of all, she had lost her one dearest hope, her most private dream which had buoyed her along for so many years. Wherever she went she had looked for him, around every corner, in every new place.

She had finally found her brother, after all the hoping and searching, only to lose him again. His eyes, green like her own, were dead to her. He did not see that she was his little sister. To the Dragon Kareem had become, she existed solely as prey. Her brother was now a cold, cruel stranger named Jah, who had forgotten the good and honest ways of the old ones.

The endless desert sands stretched before her and behind her, unreal in the strange light of the red moon that had begun to rise round and full above them. Like her, the desert was empty. Filled with nothing. Maybe that was how the darkness took you, she thought, by removing your will to live, to hope, to dream.

She closed her eyes, and when she opened them she saw a light moving in the darkness far, far away across the endlessly expanding desert. A shooting star, she thought, and remembered how the old ones made the sign of the spiral in homage to the dead soul rising to the heavens. But as she stared, she saw that the star had not just disappeared from the sky as a shooting star, but glimmered in the glow of the rising red moon. She blinked, her eyes on the moon.

Red moon rising.

She had seen a moon like that in her dream of the Empress. *Look to your dreams and follow the signs,* Calliope had said. She had to go to that place through the glimmering lights. It called her, its energy humming toward her in the empty desert darkness. She felt that strange tingling in her forehead that signaled a surge of power, and in that instant a renewed feeling of strength, of vigor and purpose, filled her. And she knew, without knowing how but with certainty, that Niko would be there waiting for her. It was up to her to find him and the Bearer to complete the circle of three, which would one day be nine.

Excerpt from *The Secret in the Stones: Tales of the Nine Charms, Book 2*

Published by Dell Yearling
an imprint of Random House Children's Books
a division of Random House, Inc.
1540 Broadway
New York, New York 10036
Reprinted by arrangement with Dell Yearling

After the girls left, Walker slipped into the clothes Elyana had given him. She'd found them in an old white trunk that was so covered in dust that when she lifted the lid, all three of them coughed. Walker had no idea what to expect, but even he had to admit that the white silk tunic and pants were exceptionally well made and obviously expensive. He knew he ought to sleep, but he was overtired and his mind full of all that had happened.

Absently he wandered around the room, listening to the wind gust around the tower. He thought of how his dog, Blue, was always spooked by the wind, and a wave of homesickness washed over him. He wondered for the millionth time if he'd ever get home again. He wouldn't even mind being at the museum on the field trip that had started this whole thing, listening to boring old "Hoot Owl" Hamilton, his teacher, talking about stupid haystack paintings and the way that art dude Monet had captured the essence of light. Sighing, Walker stared down at the floor, realizing that he was standing on the mosaic of the dragon. He felt a tingle as he stood there, looking at the powerful creature frozen below him.

He bent and brushed some dust off the dragon. It was holding something in its claws, something in the very center of the circle—a square tile. Blowing the dust off that, he saw a strange triangular symbol. His eyes widened. It was the same symbol as the one on the door of the bones reader's house. What had Niko called it? The Dragon's Eye was flanked by square tiles marked with other symbols. One of them was the exact twin of his red charm. The realization was so surprising that his nose began to itch the way it did sometimes when he was concentrating. Could it be the key to something? he wondered. Was he supposed to see this mosaic? It couldn't just be a coincidence. He remembered Niko telling him that his master didn't believe in coincidence. He said all things happened for a reason. Right now, Walker, who had argued against such a nonlogical point of view, suddenly began to think that maybe, just maybe, Niko's master had been right.